SINISTER SÉANCE

Abruptly, the green light in front of Madame Swoboda went out. The darkness was total. Chairs scraped as they were pushed back. For an instant Shayne speculated on the sheer animal terror which pervaded the room, then he put his arms around Clarissa and pulled her from her chair.

There was a strange "punging" sound, then a clatter.

A match was struck and the tiny flame of a candle grew in the dark. Madame Swoboda screamed. She stood in the flickering light, her eyes fixed on the candle.

It was black. A black candle was for death . . . and on the floor lay the knife that had been thrown for the killing. . . .

Dolls
Are
Deadly

Brett Halliday

A DELL BOOK

For Helen Kasson
and Ryerson Johnson

Published by
DELL PUBLISHING CO., INC.
1 Dag Hammarskjold Plaza
New York, New York 10017

1

Michael Shayne stared dreamily from his office window, his chair at a nearly impossible tilt and his big feet scuffing the desk top. A close-burning cigarette warmed the knobby fingers of his right hand. Four fingers of his other hand warmed a glass of Hennessy. The cognac was good for a while yet, but the hot end of the cigarette was getting uncomfortably close to his fingers.

He had three choices.

He could swing his feet to the floor so he could reach the ash tray on the desk. He could try flipping the butt in from where he sat. Or he could drop it on the floor. He pushed the burning end of the cigarette out from his fingers another sixteenth of an inch while he pondered the alternatives. The second choice was adventurous and the third was easy—but Lucy Hamilton, his petite, brown-haired secretary whose typewriter was busily going in the front office, wouldn't approve of either.

Shayne decided to do it the hard way.

He took a sip from the glass, swung his long legs to the floor, reached to the ash tray and thumbed out the cigarette. A breeze from the open window sifted through his red hair. The breeze smelled of the sea and he thought of his little Cuban friend, Sylvester, out there on it somewhere, his party-boat solid under his feet, and nothing but clean air and sky and water around him. Sylvester had no troubles. His boat was paid for and he ran it where and when he pleased.

Shayne's heavy brows quirked upward and his lips compressed as he indulged in a moment of rare musing. "When I was picking out a profession what in hell made me think I wanted to be a private detective? I should have been a charter-boat captain. Everything clean and pleasant—and safe. I could be home every night. Lucy would approve."

The redhead took another pull at the cognac. It would be good on the water today. Hot and cold by turns, invigorating and restful—like a Turkish bath. All this and a fishing pole bending double while the reel made shrill music as a marlin hit the mackerel bait and ran it out two hundred yards for the first jump.

Shayne looked at his watch. Though it was not yet noon it was late to start out, except that it wasn't entirely the sport that he went for. Just to be on the untroubled water was enough. He had been going out on Sylvester's boat for years off and on, and though months would go by sometimes, when he went down again it was the same. Sylvester's wide Cuban grin made him welcome and they picked up where they had left off. The little, round, uncalculating man with the shining black eyes was as refreshing as the salt spray. Childlike and honest, he had a loyalty to Shayne and a liking as deep as the ocean on which he made his living. His fisherman's hands were calloused, but his soul was not.

Shayne made his decision and reached for the phone, then stopped midway. There was no use calling. If Sylvester's boat had been chartered today it would be out already, and if it hadn't the little Cuban would be only too glad to take it out at any hour for his old friend.

Through the open door Shayne could see the back of Lucy's head. "I'm going fishing, angel," he said lazily.

She stopped typing and swung her chair around. "It's pretty hot for a nighthawk. Sure you won't get sunstroke?"

"I never got it from you—not quite."

"I'm nothing like the sun." She smiled across at him.

"You are, exactly—when you smile."

Shayne finished the cognac, got up and reached for his hat on top of a filing cabinet. In the act of putting it on, however, he saw the knob to the outside door turn, so instead of leaving he shut the door between the outside office and his own, walked to the cooler and filled a glass with water and drank it. Then he returned to his desk, took a half-empty bottle of Hennessy from the bottom drawer and poured three more fingers of cognac. Easing himself to the chair, he lifted his feet to the desk top again. While he sipped the drink he listened to the pleasing murmur of Lucy's voice until it was all

7

but drowned out by a hoarse insistent bass. A moment after, as he knew it would, a knock sounded at the door of his inner office and even before he said, "Come in," the door was opened by Lucy.

At first glance Shayne didn't like the looks of the man who loomed over her shoulder. At second glance he knew why. He recognized him—Henry Henlein, a confirmed mobster, a "muscleman" who made his living by playing his fists over faces, and sometimes a switchblade, and sometimes a broken bottle or beer stein—or half a brick. "Henny" was versatile. He was also durable. For more years than the law of averages allows, to say nothing of man-made law, he had hired out for the fast and dirty dollar to a succession of Miami crime bosses.

Shayne's gray eyes were cold as he pointedly looked past the man to Lucy. "I'm busy, Miss Hamilton." He turned his glance to the wispy clouds in the sky outside the window. He liked the view better there.

"Mr. Henry Henlein insists on seeing you," Lucy said in equally as cold a voice.

Still looking out the window, Shayne said with deceptive gentleness, "Henny's probably collecting for the Private Investigator's Protective Association. Tell him I'll protect myself. Tell him if he's still there when I turn around I'll break his arm across your typewriter. Tell him I'll snap his fingers one at a time and lay his face open to the bone with my leather gloves that I soak in salt water and dry out fast so the seams are like knives."

Shayne's sarcasm was lost on the muscleman. "You got it all wrong, Mr. Shayne," he protested. "I'm here like anyone else, to hire a detective. I need one bad."

"I don't need the business bad." Shayne took a slow sip of brandy.

"Look, Mr. Shayne," Henlein said, his voice rising, "you're a private eye, ain't you? Well, I got something that needs looking at."

The voice carried such a hoarse and curious urgency that Shayne turned reluctantly from the window to survey the hoodlum. Henry Henlein topped Lucy by half a foot. He was heavy-boned and thick-waisted and going a little to pot. His faded blond hair started low on his forehead and the Miami sun had not been kind to his desiccated skin; it was blotched and red. Even if Shayne hadn't known who the man was or how he made his living, he'd have been repelled by the gross brutality on the loose-lipped face.

There was a peculiar sort of irony, Shayne thought, in the difference between the punishment the law exacted and that which racketeering crime lords did. While the offender against the law often escaped with nothing worse than a short jail sentence, the offender against illegal syndicate activities usually ended up maimed or dead. As a result, musclemen and enforcers for gangsters were seldom out of work.

"I'll say it once more." Shayne spoke with morose disinterest. "I'm busy. And I expect to be busy for a long time."

9

The hoodlum's hand jerked toward the glass of brandy which Shayne held. "Yeh, I can see you are." The wry observation indicated an inordinate show of intelligence for Henlein who was rated, even by those who hired him, as "strong back, dim brain."

Henlein shouldered past Lucy, scuffed across the room and lowered himself to the edge of the chair beside Shayne's desk. "It won't take you but a second," he said in a voice that was, strangely, almost pleading, "to see what I came to show you."

For the first time Shayne turned his full attention on the man. His gray eyes narrowed and his fingers lifted to pull gently at his left earlobe.

This hoodlum was terrified! His thick lower lip drooped like that of an imbecile, revealing ground-down, tobacco-stained teeth, and his milk-blue eyes were vacant of everything except fear.

Shayne's big feet, still propped on the desk, were in Henny's line of vision. The hoodlum stood up, his hand digging into the side coat pocket of his blue pin-striped suit, and lifted out the last thing Shayne would have expected—a doll.

Reaching across Shayne's long legs, he placed the doll in the middle of the desk. It was about four inches tall, made of hopsacking with black yarn hair and the semblance of eyes, nose and mouth stitched on in the same black yarn. It was stabbed through the chest with a black-headed pin.

"Voodoo doll," Shayne said idly. "What public spirited citizen sent you this, Henny?"

"That's what I want you to find out, Mr. Shayne."

The redhead took a sip of brandy, unwound his

legs slowly and swung them to the floor. He put the glass down, reached out with one long, knobby finger and pushed the pin deeper into the doll.

Henlein's quick intake of breath made a small rasping noise. "Don't do that!"

"Why not?"

"Because it's 'sposed to be me, see? Somebody wants to kill me." Henlein disgorged the words as if the thought were beyond belief, but the sweat on his face and his terrified eyes showed that he believed it nevertheless.

Shayne said dryly, "I can't imagine why anybody would want you harmed, Henny."

"Neither can I. But you gotta find out who does."

The redhead shrugged. "As long as the curse is already on you, I guess I can't help."

"You can find out who sent it," Henlein exploded. "You're a detective, serving the public. I'm part of the public. I got money to pay."

"I couldn't be less interested in what happens to your kind," Shayne said coldly and turned back to the window.

"Whadda ya mean, my kind?" The hoodlum bristled. "I'm human, ain't I? If someone kills me he's got to take the rap the same's if he killed you —or—ah—the President of the United States." It was deep thinking for Henny Henlein and his acned forehead wrinkled with the effort.

"Not unless he gets caught."

"That's the point. I want to hire you to catch him."

"Before or after?"

"Look, Mr. Shayne, this might be funny to you—" the muscleman ran a thick tongue over his dry lips—"but it ain't to me. Whoever it was sent me *two* dolls. Here's the other one. With a noose!"

Henlein removed a second doll from his pocket and laid it carefully on the desk as if he felt that this construction of cloth and yarn which symbolized his body were actually a part of it. His hand shook as he drew it back.

The redhead picked up the second doll. Except for the noose with the seven-times-around hangman's knot, made with the common sort of heavy brown twine department stores use to tie boxes, this doll was identical to the first—crudely made, stuffed with a sort of cellulose which, at one loose seam, was visible; the yarn hair ragged and carelessly applied; the eyes, nose and mouth formed with only a few deft stitches.

He put it down, saying, "The only way it can hurt you is if you die of fright. You afraid of little dolls, Henny?"

"It ain't the dolls, I told you. It's the guy who sent them."

"Well, why don't you work him over? Break his jaw, cave in some ribs, give him the knee! You're a muscleman, aren't you?"

"I don't know who sent them!" Henlein shouted. "If I knew would I be here wasting my time?"

"Probably not. Don't waste any more. I won't take the case."

Shayne lit a cigarette, coolly blowing smoke just

past Henlein's face. There was sardonic humor in the idea of a professional killer trying to hire a detective to protect him against the sender of a couple of tiny dolls. Although Henlein's fear was genuine, the situation was too incongruous to seem real. If it should be something more than a morbid prank, however, then sending the dolls had been a sly stroke on someone's part, for this was a kind of menace outside Henlein's experience. A "do this or else" threat he could have taken in his stride. A beating with a lead-filled sap or a gun barrel he could understand. The threat of annihilation with gun lead he could have brushed off. But this mysterious way of heralding murder, these dolls with their other-world implications, were terrifying to his dim, slow-witted brain.

Henny Henlein's stupidity was known to mobsters and police alike. He did what he was told to do like a robot, but in any situation requiring thought he was lost. His head, like his body, was only fat, muscle and bone. His bosses didn't often trust him with a gun, unless they told him exactly what to do with it, but the police, and others who had reason to be interested, were convinced that some of his muscular activity had added up to murder. The only way he had beaten these raps was by staying mute and letting the mob's mouthpiece talk for him.

Henlein shook his head in genuine puzzlement. Suddenly something like a ray of hope crossed his heavy features. "I know what's eating on you,

13

Shayne. You been hearing too many stories about me. Lies. All lies. I never gunned nobody in my life. I'm a muscleman, not a enforcer. See?"

"There's a difference?" Shayne asked sourly.

"Hell, yes. I only move around, collecting, and like that for legitimate rackets, and maybe 'working' somebody once in a while that gets out of line, ya know?"

"What's the difference if you kill a man quick or cripple him so he dies slowly?"

"Huh?" Henlein stared vacantly. "Look, Mr. Shayne, I'll pay. Plenty." His hand moved to his breast pocket and came out with a fistful of green. "I'm working for D. L. now. I'm rolling in it."

"Keep rolling. I don't want it."

"Don't want—money?" The hoodlum's mouth opened in stark disbelief. "You gotta take it!"

"I don't *have* to do anything," Shayne snapped, "especially work for one of De Luca's hoods. I've never liked the loan-shark racket and I like the hired thugs who go around beating up idiots who can't pay his usurious rates even less."

"That ain't what I do for D. L. I only collect—"

"I know. Blood or money."

"It ain't that way. It's a legitimate racket."

Shayne swung out of his chair, walked to the door and held it open. "You rather go out by the window, Henlein? It's three floors to Flagler."

Henlein rose reluctantly and walked slowly past Shayne. He seemed to have shrunk since he came in and deep lines had formed beside his mouth. At the door he made a final, despairing effort. "Think

14

about it, Mr. Shayne. Please! Whatever you say, I'll pay. If you change your mind give me a call. At D. L.'s will get me."

"I won't change my mind." Shayne moved along with him to the outer door.

"Look, Mr. Shayne," Henlein began accusingly, "if anything happens to me—"

The redhead pushed him through the door and shut it.

Lucy stopped typing and looked up reproachfully. "How could you turn him down, Michael? I don't care who he is, that poor man was terrified."

Shayne said tightly, "I draw the line, Lucy, at keeping a professional murderer from being murdered. I know the law doesn't, but I have a code of ethics which I don't think it would hurt the law to embrace."

"Even so, he's human—"

"That's what he claimed. I'm inclined to doubt it."

"Sometimes I wonder whether you are. It's only human to make an effort to keep a man from being killed."

"Lucy, do you have any conception of what that man does to make a living, day in and day out? He breaks bones like you do pencil leads, coldly and deliberately. Nothing I charged him with in there was exaggerated. It would nauseate you if I went into detail. Anyhow, why so indignant?" Shayne bent, resting his cheek on Lucy's hair. "Don't tell me you believe in those little dolls."

She softened. "Not exactly. But someone sends

them and that someone *wishes* you dead, and if he wishes hard enough and long enough, maybe you will be!"

"Nothing surer than that," the redhead agreed, "except taxes. And they don't need wishing either. I'm going fishing, angel."

Lucy sniffed and went back to her typing.

2

Shayne stopped off at his apartment on the Miami River and changed to polo shirt and sneakers. The sun was hot, but there was a breeze coming in from the ocean that would be even cooler on the water. As he drove across the Causeway to the Beach, he wound down the windows in the car and let the wind blow through his red hair. Fishing was going to be good today.

As always, once he had crossed from Miami proper, he felt the spirit of holiday around him. The Spanish moss waved with carnival gaiety and the meticulously tended flowers around the winter houses made brilliant spots of color in the sun. Shayne followed a line of royal palms and whistled a soundless tune as he turned his car south on the Beach. Drawing into a parking space at the head of a wharf, he cut the engine. His pulse quickened pleasurably as he sighted the *Santa Clara* still at her berth and Sylvester out on deck in the act of casting off. He had arrived at exactly the right time.

As the redhead moved swiftly down the wharf in his long-legged stride, Sylvester sighted him. Dropping the rope he held, the rotund little Cuban waved wildly and, taking off from the boat's gunnel landed precariously on the edge of the wharf, caught his balance and scurried excitedly to meet Shayne.

Suddenly, however, his face took on a woeful look, as if he had just remembered something. "Mike, I am so sorry. I know I tell you to come any time. Any time you would be welcome, but today—"

"That's all right, Sylvester. Is the *Santa Clara* chartered?"

The little party-boat skipper nodded sadly.

Shayne dropped his big hand to Sylvester's shoulder. "Don't worry about it. I should have called. Another time, *amigo*."

"But come to the boat a minute," Sylvester pleaded. "Meet my friends—"

"Not now. You go ahead. Catch the tide."

"Sylvester!" a hearty voice shouted from the deck. "What's holding us up?"

A man, clad only in white trousers and a white fisherman's hat, had appeared from within the cabin. He held a highball glass in one hand and a thick cigar in the other. Though his body ran to fat there was the suggestion of muscle underneath.

"*Uno momento,* please, *Señor* Ed," Sylvester called back. "My old friend, Mike, is here."

Señor Ed was joined by another man carrying a highball. "So say hello to your friend and let's get going," he said proprietarily. He was younger than the first man and wore dark glasses and a lavishly colored Hawaiian sport shirt. He took a swallow of

18

the highball. "Red snapper run on the tide, don't they?"

In the middle of one of the world's best game-fish areas, these men were going out hand-lining for meat fish! It seemed slightly ridiculous.

"Everything set, Vince?" a third voice called from within the awning-covered cockpit.

"Everything but Sylvester," the man in the Hawaiian shirt said dryly. "He's reviving an old friendship."

"What the hell, Sylvester!" The third man poked his head into view, raising himself from one of the built-in benches along the rail. "Get the lead out! Cast off and let's go!"

Sylvester looked across at them, tugging at the shapeless skipper's cap which rode jauntily on the side of his head. "*Señores*," he pleaded, "you have been so good to me. One thing more I ask. My friend, Mike, he is old, good friend. Can he go too?"

"No, Sylvester," the redhead said. "Another time. They've got you chartered." He started to leave, but the little Cuban grasped his arm firmly.

"Wait, Mike. Let them answer. They will want you, I know."

The three men on the boat exchanged questioning glances, then Ed, the man who had spoken first, said in his hearty voice, "Sure, Sylvester. The more the merrier."

"*Gracias!*" Sylvester's round, perspiring face beamed. "You will not be sorry. Mike good fisherman . . . good drinker. . . ."

"Well, there's plenty of liquor," Ed shouted.

Shayne still held back, reluctant to intrude on a private party, but Sylvester tugged at him, looking up into the lean, hard-jawed face with almost the pride of a mother. "Is all right, Mike. They want you. I want you. Everybody want you." He lowered his voice. "They charter my boat for three weeks now—steady. They have such a good time on the *Santa Clara*. And wait till I show you what they done. My best friends—next to you, Mike."

When he had pulled Shayne to the boat and watched him step across, he stooped, loosened the rope from the mooring post and tossed it aboard. "Mike, meet Ed and Vince and Slim Collins."

Shayne shook hands all around. "This is mighty good of you."

"Any friend of Sylvester's is a friend of ours," Ed said expansively. His chunky face was burned and peeling, as were his shoulders. The Miami sun was no kinder to his blond skin than it was to Henny Henlein's, Shayne noted, and wondered why thoughts of the frightened mobster should intrude just then. Ed's head was burned too. He was bald except for a circle of grayish-black fuzz around the back of his head which gave the impression of a misplaced angel's halo.

Vince, the younger man in the loud Hawaiian shirt, put a highball glass into Shayne's hand. He was swarthy-faced and thick-bodied, with hair as black as a Cuban's and black restless eyes which never seemed to stop moving. Lifting his glass, he said, "Here's bait in your box."

Shayne took a deep swallow, repressing a shudder as it went down. He looked over at the low, built-in table in the cockpit's stern. On it was an ice bucket, a bottle of water and a bottle of rum, labeled *Demerara*.

Slim, the third man, had stretched out again on the kapok cushions on the bench near the table, his glass on the floor beside him and his hat half over his eyes. Intercepting Shayne's glance at the rum bottle, he grinned. "If you're a drinking man, like Sylvester claims, then you know Demerara."

"I know it. It's better than a hundred and fifty proof."

"Yeah. Gets you where you want to go fast. I can't drink it ashore. Knocks me off my feet. But out here on the water it seems just right."

Slim's complexion was swarthy too. He looked Sicilian or Italian, or maybe Portuguese. Sylvester had called him Collins, which didn't seem to fit at all, but he came honestly by his first name anyhow. He was painfully tall and gangling, with a stooped posture which called attention to the fact that he was no longer young. He had dark eyes which he kept half-closed, and large, widely separated front teeth.

"Sylvester," he called lazily. "How's your drink holding out?"

"I'll take him one," Ed said.

He poured Demerara in a glass without measuring, added a dollop of water and a single ice cube. It was a drink to stagger a horse, but when he handed it to Sylvester at the wheel, the little man

21

grinned and lapped it all down. Ed took the empty glass, refilled it from the bottle and returned to Sylvester. "Not so fast on this one, fella. Get us out of the harbor first."

Sylvester laughed. "Don' worry, my frien'. Dead drunk I could navigate. With the engine you gave me, in a good boat like the *Santa Clara*, a baby could run her." He swallowed half the glassful and when Ed moved back to the stern, beckoned to Shayne.

Thoughtfully, the redhead moved over to the wheelhouse.

"Mike, you know what?" Sylvester whispered. "They have such a good time on the *Santa Clara*, they buy her a new engine! A gift to me. They even dirty it up so I wouldn't have to pay more property tax. Is new, expensive engine—Gray Marine—but looks old. Fools the tax collector." He laughed again, in childish delight.

"Give it to me slow," Shayne said. "You never saw these men until a few weeks ago, but they dug into their pockets and bought you a new engine—just because they like you?"

"Tha's what I been trying to tell you, Mike."

"Was the old engine bad?"

"Not bad, not good." Sylvester shrugged. "But this one the best. Slim even work on to it to supercharge it some. He is expert mechanic. Now this engine lift the *Santa Clara* like a flying fish out of the water. After a while maybe I show you, if they let me. They don't like for me to let it out. What for a fast engine if you don't go fast, Mike?"

22

"That's a good question." Shayne massaged his left earlobe gently. "Is this Slim a mechanic at home?" Where would a mechanic get the money to come to Florida on an extended vacation and, further, engage in such altruism?

"Is hobby mechanic," Sylvester said. "Do-it-yourself man, he says. To make money he is a contractor. Very rich. They are all rich. To them to buy a new engine the expense is nothing. Still"—his round face sobered—"how many rich men would do such a nothing? I am most lucky."

"Looks that way." Shayne rubbed his lean jaw thoughtfully.

With its V-bottomed hull and narrower-than-ordinary stern, Sylvester's boat had been faster than it needed to be for fishing, before. He had never outgrown a boyish passion for speed, and had been willing to sacrifice a little pay-load for it. But now it had the new engine that could "lift the *Santa Clara* out of the water" bought for him by strangers who liked him and had dirtied it up "to fool the tax collector." But they didn't want him to speed with it. Why? Why, even, had they bought it for him?

Shayne walked back to join the men in the canopied cockpit.

"Help yourself, Mike." Ed waved cordially toward the bottle. "Drink and be merry. Today's a holiday."

"Any special one?" Shayne poured a generous glass, but set it down untouched.

"Since we three got together we declare a holiday every day," Slim said lazily.

"You didn't know each other before you came to Miami?"

"No. Damnedest thing. Never met till about a month ago. In a bar on Flagler the first day I arrived. But the minute we met, we clicked. We'd all come down to live it up and fish, and we were lucky enough to find Sylvester. . . . Hey, Sylvester! How's your drink coming?"

"She's all gone."

"Can't have that." Ed walked over with the bottle and poured straight rum over the melting ice in Sylvester's glass.

Shayne said pleasantly, "Quite a coincidence, your hitting it off so well. From your accents, I'd say you're from different parts of the country."

"Couldn't be differenter," Slim said. "I'm from Philly and Ed's from Detroit. In the insurance business there. Vince here's from Arizona. Got him a motel chain. Down here we all got beach cabanas. Vince claims some of his in Arizona can match them at a fourth the price but, what the hell—money's to spend, or what good is it?"

Shayne took a cautious swallow of the rum. "You're all down here alone?"

"All but Ed. He brought his wife."

Ed had come back from tending to Sylvester's drink and was refilling his own. "I'm practically alone," he said cheerfully. "When she isn't playing canasta, she's shopping."

Shayne sat down, relaxed with his long legs sprawled out, and watched the shore recede. Already the beach was only a thin line, and the palms behind it a hedgelike, hazy green. A small yacht passed with two men and two women sitting at an umbrella-covered table sipping drinks. Ed and Slim shouted across the water and waved. The men on the yacht stared impassively, but the women— young, lithe and blond—looked interestedly at the boatload of men and waved back.

They were getting into the Gulf Stream now with little whirlpools showing everywhere and yellow gulfweed floating in patches. There were bursts of flying-fish in the air, with boilings in the water as a bigger fish pursued them.

"You want to try for a barracuda, Mike?" Sylvester called. "I'll put the mullet strips on for you."

"I'll take the wheel, Sylvester," Vince offered.

Vince set down his drink and walked over. Shayne looked back. Through the screen which covered the wheelhouse window he could see Vince in his flamboyant shirt bent over the compass and some charts, his hand resting with easy familiarity on the wheel. For a motel mogul from landlocked Arizona, this man seemed inordinately good on a boat. He seemed inordinately sober too, despite all the high-voltage rum being passed around.

In contrast to his steadiness, Sylvester lurched from the cabin, weaving unsteadily and grinning foolishly. He made his way precariously to the bait box aft, took out the prepared mullet strips, baited three hooks and gave them to Shayne. The redhead let them troll back in the boat's wake.

"Use the fishing chair if you want," Ed drawled. "We're too lazy to do any fishing that takes energy. Better strap yourself in against the big ones."

Shayne shook his head. "With light six-thread I'm not looking for anything big enough to pull me overboard."

"We aren't looking for anything, period. After a while, if we anchor, we might put out some hand lines—and hope the fish won't latch onto 'em." He laughed. "Mostly we just like to get out here and drink on the water."

This was about as screwy a fishing party as Shayne had ever chummed up with.

"Is like a club, Mike," Sylvester explained. "All nice and happy. They get along with everybody."

As though to prove the statement, Slim raised himself on his elbow from the kapok cushions and waved genially at a police boat that was passing. The men on the boat waved back, the one at the wheel tooting twice in recognition of Sylvester's boat. Sylvester had run a charter boat off Miami for many years and the happy little Cuban was a favorite of everybody's.

Shayne's bait was trolling nicely, bouncing on the swell. The water was silver-blue and the breeze just cool enough to compensate for the hot sun. It was a good day. The redhead leaned back, listening to the cheerful banter between Sylvester and the three men. The rum was disappearing steadily; the humor and the laughter gaining weight and volume. A carefree holiday seemed to be the only thing on anybody's mind.

26

Shayne felt a tug on his line that communicated through his hands clear up into his shoulders. His star-drag reel whirred as a fish ran out the line, and he experienced the sharp, familiar feel of satisfaction the weight of a fighting fish always gave him. No one except Sylvester seemed much interested as he played the fish and reeled it in. It was an eight-pound barracuda, evil-looking, its long jaws lined with razor-sharp teeth.

"I've caught 'em eight feet long," Sylvester bragged. "Those big ones can eat a man's leg off." He moved drunkenly, taking the fish from the hook and packing it in ice, a necessary precaution, since the flesh of a barracuda spoils more rapidly than most other tropical fish.

"Got a feeling you're going to do all the fishing that's done today, Mike," Slim said. "We started drinking too early, I guess. Fishing just seems like too much work." He started singing in a hoarse and off-key voice.

Shayne put his troll bait out again. They were well out to sea with the smooth flow of the Gulf Stream around them, and Miami an unreal wonderland vanishing in the afternoon haze. The others were quieter now. Had the calm of the open ocean finally penetrated their overstimulated senses, or had the abandoned holiday mood been put on partly for Shayne's benefit, to make him feel at ease because Sylvester had practically forced them into allowing him to join their party?

The redhead played another barracuda and lost him, then landed a good-sized grouper. When Sylvester came over to take it off the hook he rose, saying casually, "I've had enough for a while."

He sauntered along the deck, went down three steps and entered the cabin, where he walked over and lifted the hatch on the engine housing. The new engine looked powerful. As Sylvester had said, it had been dirtied and smeared with oil. It took close inspection to tell that it was new. The red-head looked down at it for a long time, his gray eyes thoughtful.

At a chorus of shouting outside, he closed the hatch, turned away from the engine and went up on deck. They were all on the port side, craning to look ahead at another boat coming into view. Sylvester held a pair of binoculars on her.

"She's a Cuban!" he yelled.

Vince, still at the wheel, headed toward the approaching boat. At the change in direction, Sylvester came alive, set down the binoculars and picked up his drink in an unsteady hand, liquor slopping over the sides.

"Not that way," he shouted. "Fish no good that way. I take you to better place."

"Let him alone, Silvy," Ed said. "Vince is a frustrated mariner at heart. Just wants to take us for a ride. And who knows, might be some *señoritas* on the boat if she's Cuban." He laughed boisterously. "I'd rather fish for *señoritas* than fish for fish."

"What is that—fustrated?" Sylvester asked.

"*Frus*trated. Means wants to do something, but don't get a chance."

"Ho!" The little Cuban laughed loudly, pounding one thick, hairy hand on his leg. "I know wha tha's like. When I walk on Collins Avenue and see the girls. All the girls I can't have. . . . Lettim alone then."

Vince brought the *Santa Clara* in close, deftly heeling to port beside a thirty-foot power boat named *La Ballena*.

"The Whale!" Sylvester yelled. "Cuban whale!"

The ocean top in the Stream was flat as a table.

From *La Ballena* came wild Cuban music. On deck, a girl clad in short red shorts and the suggestion of a red bra was rhumbaing, her inky hair flying, her teeth, eyes and earrings flashing. A young, dark man sat on the rail watching her and shouting encouragement in Spanish. As the music increased in tempo, her movements grew more abandoned. Then, abruptly, the record player stopped. Inertia kept her moving for a moment in the new silence, then she too stopped, looking up startled at the nearness of the *Santa Clara*.

Two older men who had fish lines out, looked around.

"You folks fishin' or funnin'?" Ed shouted.

"A little of both," the taller man said.

"Is there any difference?" his companion asked.

Although the men did not look alike, they both had full, loosely-put-together faces and their eyes, despite the bantering words, held a certain flint. They wore light, broad-brimmed Panama straws and spoke with a slight accent.

"Why don't you join us, *señores?*"

The girl leaned on the rail smiling, her coal-black

29

eyes with dilated pupils resting with frank feminine appraisal on Shayne. *"Si,* why don't you?" Her low, throbbing voice had a strong Spanish accent.

"I don't rhumba," Shayne said.

"You don't have to." Her dewy eyes framed in black lashes almost reached across to him. Her breasts swelled above the red bra. Unexpectedly, she pursed her full lips into kiss-shape and leaned toward Shayne. After a moment she withdrew, humming almost silently, and moved in a slow nautch-like dance, her hips swaying provocatively, the muscles in her diaphragm moving sinuously in the bare space between the skimpy bra and the short shorts.

"I'd sure like to come aboard," Ed said regretfully, "but I promised the old lady I'd be home tonight—with fish. And I haven't done any fishing, except in Demerara."

"What kind of fish, pop?" the dark young man asked brashly. "Maybe in Cuban waters we catch some different kinds which she never taste."

"Don't matter which kind," Ed said.

"All right. You want fresh bonito? Very good baked in oven with onions and peppers around him." The young man had the same black, untamed eyes and heavy accent as the girl.

"I don't think she ever had bonito." Ed turned to Shayne. "What you going to do with your fish, Mike?"

"I don't want them," the redhead said.

"O.K., *amigo,*" Ed called. "We'll swap you a barracuda or a grouper."

"No need to swap. We give you the bonito."

"No," Sylvester insisted. "Swap is fair."

"I would love the barracuda," the girl said.

"Good. The barracuda then." The young man grinned. "It is more favored in our country than in yours."

"Your mother can cook it for us, José," the girl said. "She has most good recipe for barracuda."

Sylvester laughed thickly and clapped Shayne on the shoulder. "Tha's what I like about these boys. Every time we go out we make new friends." He lurched toward the Cuban boat and Shayne grasped his arm to keep him from falling.

The boats were close, rising gently on the swell. The young man extended his hand and grasped Sylvester's. They braced themselves and pulled, and slowly the boats drew together.

"Hey," Sylvester yelled, "now I can't let go to get the fish."

The girl laughed, looked at Shayne and languidly stretched her arm toward him. The redhead took her slim, brown hand in his own big one.

"You can let go now," she said softly to Sylvester.

Shayne felt her fingers tightening and loosening in his grasp, and the warmth flowing from her flesh.

"It is a marriage," she said, "of the moment."

Shayne smiled. It was a good moment.

Sylvester returned with the barracuda and handed it across, then took the bonito. It was a plump fish, a good ten pounds. Ed bore it away to put it on ice. The taller of the Cuban men leaned close and dropped a handful of cigars aboard the

Santa Clara. "Good *Vuelta* leaf Havana. You like."

"Is time to part," the girl said sadly.

"*Uno momento,*" the young man called. "Our ice all melt. You have enough to spare for our drinks till we get back to Cuba?"

"*Si.*" Sylvester weaved to the table, grabbed the ice bucket and lifted it across into the hands of the young man. "Keep it. The bucket too."

"*Gracias, señores.*"

Certainly there had been nothing but good will and friendly feeling expressed on all sides here. Still, something about Sylvester's gift of the ice cubes troubled the redhead. He couldn't put his finger on it, but it was there—a nagging little inconsistency.

The girl squeezed Shayne's hand convulsively and then released it, letting her fingers trail lingeringly across his palm as the boats drifted apart. When the chasm between them was a boat's width she blew him a kiss.

The engine of *La Ballena* started and, with it, the music blared forth again. The girl moved her nude shoulders and wheeled her bare knees in the nautch-like circle that carried her hips along in a seductive rhythm. As the space between the boats widened, she swirled toward the center of the deck and started again on the mad, compulsive rhumba. The music grew fainter with distance but the dance grew wilder, her movements more unrestrained. Suddenly, the young man leaped toward her and took her in his arms. They kissed in the hot, bright sunlight, her body still moving sensually against him.

The tempo of the music quickened. Still holding the kiss, he moved her backward to the companionway which led below.

On the *Santa Clara* all but Vince, who was at the wheel, had been watching. Sylvester sighed heavily. "It took him a long time. Even I—fus-trated—whatever you call it—and at my old age, would have done it sooner. And you, Michael Shayne—" he poked an unsteady finger at the rangy redhead— "would have done it on the first note."

"Michael Shayne?" Ed repeated quickly. He looked at Shayne, as did Slim and Vince, from the wheelhouse. "You mean," Ed said with no unsteadiness in his voice, "you're Michael Shayne, the private detective?"

"The same," Sylvester said proudly. "My friend, he is famous everywhere."

"Well, I'm damned!" Ed smoothed his angel's halo of graying hair. "Miami's best-known detective on our boat. Wait'll I tell the folks back home."

"Better keep it under your hat," Slim advised. "They'll think your wife put him on your tail."

"My friend, Mike, he does not tail." Sylvester straightened with drunken dignity. "My friend, Mike, he *heads* the big cases." He roared loudly at the pun.

"Like murder and such?" Ed asked, adding recklessly, "We've drunk to everything else today. Let's have a drink to murder!"

It was as if the words were prophetic. Vince had the radio tuned in to a station in Miami. The local news was on. Shayne had been hearing the droning voice only as background sound, then suddenly the newscaster's words jumped acutely into his consciousness.

"... *the body of Henry 'Henny' Henlein, behind a pile of dirt at the site of the excavation on Washington. Henlein has a long criminal record, has been arrested many times, but never convicted on a major charge. A certain mystery surrounds the slaying. Death came apparently as a result of a gunshot through the heart, but around the neck of the body there was a piece of rope—a noose tied in a hangman's knot. It has not yet been determined ...*"

Vince cut the radio off and there was only the muted roaring of the new engine as it thrust the *Santa Clara* through the empty expanse of water toward the Beach.

3

Shayne stood very still in the silence after Vince snapped off the newscast, three vertical lines deepening in his forehead.

He lit a cigarette and walked to the rail, tossing the match overboard into the water. So, after all, Henlein's fear had been justified. He had been murdered precisely as he had been afraid he would be—and within hours after he had left Shayne's office.

Lucy was going to look very accusing about this. Even so, the redhead had no regrets for having refused aid to the hoodlum. The world would have one less law-breaker in it, that was all. However, Shayne did have an absorbing curiosity as to what lay beneath the surface. Who had killed Henlein and why? Those two little dolls didn't add up to mob murder—unless something novel had been added to mob methods in Miami lately.

He turned sharply at a raucous sound. Sylvester lay prone on the bench under the starboard rail, his toes up, his wide mouth open and snoring.

"Sylvester's out," Slim called to Vince. "You'll have to take us all the way in. Can you make the channel?"

"I think so. I've watched Sylvester do it."

The sun was lowering now and the slanted afternoon light seemed to have a quieting effect on the three men. Ed took out a deck of cards and began playing solitaire. Slim, huddled in the cushions, stared glassy-eyed at the wake the boat left. The *Santa Clara,* gunning for the Beach under Vince's able handling, passed a boat which had run up its tuna flag. There were girls on it, but no one on the *Santa Clara* was showing any wolf-strain now. They all seemed tired, as though relaxing after a strenuous day of sport, which was a little peculiar, considering they hadn't roused themselves to any effort more enervating than pouring a drink. Even the rum couldn't account for all their lethargy. Sylvester had downed the biggest part of it.

As the boat sliced through the less tranquil waters near the Beach, the men stirred. Ed retrieved his bonito from the ice box and was holding it, ready to go ashore, when Vince cut the engine twenty feet out and let inertia carry them to the pier. Shayne and Slim jumped off and made the fore and aft moorings fast and put out the rubber-tire fenders.

They stood for a moment on the dock, then shook hands with Shayne—all except Ed. "My hand's fishy," he said apologetically. "You know, sometimes I wonder why I ever bring fish home. My woman won't clean them. She makes me do it and if there's anything I don't like, it's cleaning fish. For two cents I'd throw it back."

"It's sure been nice, Mr. Shayne," Vince said.

"It was nice of you to let me barge in."

"Not at all," Slim assured him. "Any time."

They hesitated, glancing over at Sylvester. "You think he'll be all right?"

Shayne nodded. "I'll carry him into the cabin. He'll sleep it off."

The three men started down the dock, waving back at Shayne, who was standing tugging at his left earlobe. They were friendly all right, as Sylvester said. Weren't they a little too friendly? Or was he too suspicious? He shrugged. That's what a lifetime of poking your nose into other people's crimes would do for you.

Still, something was bothering the redhead. It was connected in some way with the big fish Ed was so unenthusiastically carrying away. No, not that fish, the other one. The barracuda Ed had swapped to the Cubans.

Suddenly, he had it. Barracuda was the fastest spoiling fish on the coast. And they didn't have any ice on *La Ballena,* as proven by the fact that they had borrowed a bucket of cubes from Sylvester for their drinks. Without ice to hold it, the barracuda would be unfit to eat by the time they made port in Cuba. Had the Cubans known that—they must have!—and accepted the fish just out of a Latin sense of politeness, because the charter crew on Sylvester's boat had been so eager to be friendly? Or was there another reason?

A policeman moved into sight from around the dock shed. The three men had taken no more than a dozen steps from the boat. As the young cop, walking purposefully, came toward them, the men seemed to falter infinitesimally in their stride. Then Vince and Slim moved out a little ahead of Ed who was carrying the bonito and with what appeared to be studied casualness, put themselves on either side of him, almost as though they were a bodyguard. They kept moving in a sort of inverted V, came abreast of the policeman and passed him. Without giving them a glance, he continued in his positive stride straight to Shayne at the dock edge.

"You Michael Shayne?"

The cop's youth and truculence rubbed Shayne the wrong way. He nodded sourly.

"Peter Painter wants to see you."

Shayne took a pack of cigarettes from his pocket and lit one, flipping the match into the water. "Suppose I don't want to see Peter Painter?"

"It don't make any difference what you want. When a guy's found murdered with your address in his pocket, you're involved, brother."

"Don't 'brother' me! Half the people in greater Miami carry my address in their pocket."

"But half the people ain't murdered. Henny Henlein was."

"What does Painter want me to do? Send flowers? It would be a pleasure—to Henny's murderer."

The cop blinked uncertainly. "You hadn't ought to talk like that. You're in a bad enough jam as it is. And you're not helping yourself by keeping Painter waiting."

Shayne took a deep drag on the cigarette and blew out smoke. "Maybe you don't know how

38

things are between Peter Painter and me. There's nothing I'd rather do than keep him waiting—and vice versa."

The policeman stared at Shayne with the look of a boy who had been sent on a man's job. "Come on now, Mr. Shayne. I've got a job to do."

Shayne growled, "Why didn't you put it that way in the first place? Where's Painter?"

"On Washington, right off Alton—where they found Henlein's body. Painter won't let them move it till *you* get there."

"Flattering of Petey to call me in on consultation. All right, tell him I'll be there, after I've put my friend where the mosquitoes won't get him." He turned abruptly and stepped onto the boat.

When the policeman did not move, Shayne added, "Or would you rather make a real pinch and take me in handcuffed?"

"Of course not, Mr. Shayne." Now that he saw that the redhead was not going to be difficult, the policeman's manner changed. He looked toward Sylvester, saying mildly, "He looks like he's dead."

"Livest dead man you ever saw. Put your fingers in his mouth if you don't believe me. But count them first."

Scooping Sylvester up in his arms as though he were a half-grown boy, Shayne carried him down the companionway steps into the cabin and laid him on a bunk. He'd have a talk with Sylvester tomorrow, after the Cuban sobered up.

He tossed the cigarette butt into the water as he strode up the dock to his car with the young officer.

"How'd you find me? I know my office didn't give out."

"Painter put out an alert on your license number. The squad boys covering this area reported your car parked here."

Shayne grunted. "The master criminologist at his devious best."

By barreling his car all the way between lights, Shayne arrived in a dead heat with the policeman. Except at the near end where a few condemned houses still stood, the street was a pile of rubble where buildings had been razed preparatory to putting up a multiple-unit apartment building. Toward the middle of the block a mound of earth, removed in the process of replacing a water main, covered half the street. Across from it a line of cars was parked—two black police cars, the photographer's Jaguar and Peter Painter's lime-green coupé. In front of the mound of dirt two policemen stood guard to deflect the morbidly curious.

Shayne parked and strode toward the dirt pile. Painter, a small, slender man with sharp eyes and a thin black mustache, scowled and caressed his mustache with his thumbnail.

The redhead stopped, looking down at the lifeless body of Henny Henlein. Blood had seeped from a wound in his chest, staining his pin-striped coat. Around his neck, incongruously, was a hangman's noose. A few feet away a snub-nosed pocket gun with a walnut handle lay in the dirt.

Shayne stooped over the body. There was no question but that the bullet which had killed Henlein had been fired at close range. The hole in his coat was marked with powder burns. The noose around his neck was made out of common clothesline and was tied in the same hangman's knot as the noose around the neck of the tiny voodoo doll Henlein had brought to Shayne's office.

"All right, Shayne," Painter said, making his voice weary, "what's your involvement in this?"

"What makes you think I've got any?"

Painter's eyes flared. "Because it's just the kind of cockeyed murder you'd have something to do with. Look at that noose! It didn't kill him. His neck isn't even bruised. It was hung on him *after* he'd been killed. It's a symbol, or a threat, or a message to someone."

Painter was right about this anyway. The noose had probably been put around the hoodlum's neck to let someone know that he had been murdered by the same person who sent him the voodoo doll. It was like a signed card saying, "I did it." But who was it meant for? And why had Henlein been shot instead of strangled or stabbed? The other doll had had a pin through its chest. Had two people sent dolls to Henlein?

"Any other clues on him?" Shayne asked casually, wondering why Painter had not mentioned the voodoo dolls before this.

"Yes, a good one. Your name and address. What's your connection? Who killed him?"

The redhead fastened his gray eyes quizzically on Painter. "I wouldn't know. Do you? Or is that question too personal?"

41

"He had your address," Painter sputtered.

"As I told your bright young man when he came crowding me, so do half the people of greater Miami. My newspaper publicity pays off. Maybe he was going to call me, but the guy with the gun interfered." He gave Painter a wicked grin. "And now, if you'll excuse me—"

Shayne turned slowly, expecting Painter to produce the little dolls at any moment for a surprise effect and start his grilling all over again.

Painter did step in front of him, but not to produce any dolls, merely to sound a belligerent warning. "Don't get sarcastic with me, shamus. You're not above the law and my office is going to be watching you close on this. You give me the ghost of a reason and I'll have you down to headquarters so fast it'll make your teeth rattle. So now, just give me the facts. What's that noose doing around Henlein's neck?"

"How do I know? Maybe he always wears it. Look, Petey, I've got other things to do."

"Such as what?"

"It's none of your damned business." Shayne stepped around Painter and strode down the road to his car.

He slammed the door decisively, made a U-turn to head south on Alton Avenue, and sped toward the McArthur Causeway which led to the city of Miami. Once there, he stopped at the first bar he came to on Biscayne Boulevard, ordered a double brandy, carried it to a phone booth and dialed the *Daily News*. He asked for his old friend, Tim

Rourke, and after a moment the veteran reporter's voice came lazily over the wire.

"Hi, Mike. What's new?"

"That's what I called to ask you."

"Nothing much. A murder over on the Beach. A hoodlum—"

"I know about that. What else?"

"God, you're jaded. What do you want, a massacre?"

"Just some information—about that woman down by the river who's been holding seances the last month or so. Her name's Madame Swoboda."

"Yeah. She's quite a tourist attraction. I've been going to do a story on her for the paper."

"Does she sell voodoo dolls?"

"By the hundreds. Also conjure candles, love potions and goofer dust."

"What the hell is goofer dust?"

"Graveyard soil. I don't know what it's good for, but I can find out if you want some."

"Don't bother. If I ever do, I know where to get it free." Shayne finished the brandy. "One thing more, Tim. Henny Henlein was working for De Luca. Any reason you know why D. L. might want him under six feet of goofer dust?"

"Can't think of any. From what I hear, Henny was the ideal muscleman. He followed orders and he couldn't think."

"Maybe he began to *try* to think."

"Don't know why he should. D. L.'s supposed to be a good boss, as gangsters go. Even pensions 'em off—if they live that long."

"Maybe he decided to save money on one pension."

"Henny wasn't old enough to be retired. And anyway, the loan racket's booming."

"Do you think Henny got out of line and tried a speculation on his own?"

"I don't know. I'll keep an ear to the ratline though, and let you know if I hear anything."

"Thanks, Tim. I'll see you soon."

Shayne hung up, waited a moment, then raised the receiver, dropped in a coin and dialed his office number. It was after hours and he expected to get his answering service, but was pleasurably surprised to hear Lucy Hamilton's voice come musically over the wire.

"Michael Shayne's office."

"It's the man himself, in person. Has anything happened since I left?"

"Has anything happened, he asks! Has anything *not* happened. The police have been calling. That man with the little dolls has been murdered—"

"I know about that. Anything else?"

"Anything else! Yes, there is something else. You should have taken that poor man's case when he asked you to. Then maybe he wouldn't be dead now. You're just as involved as if you *had* taken it, because he had your address in his pocket—"

"I know," Shayne interrupted, "but he didn't have the two dolls."

"Of course not. *I've* got them."

"What for? Are you starting a private eye business of your own?"

"No, but he came back again after you'd left, to try and talk you into changing your mind about helping him, and left the dolls with me because I seemed interested, which is more than you did. He seemed glad to get rid of them, though he was nice about it. He said he didn't want to put the curse on me. I convinced him the curse was only dangerous for the person it was originally meant for—"

"You're not sure about that. You took an awful chance." Shayne grinned. "What's the 'something else' you mentioned that happened?"

"There's a woman here waiting to see you. That's why I couldn't close the office at a decent hour." Lucy lowered her voice. "She says she's going to wait to see you if it takes all night. She's been here about an hour and she's so fidgety she's about to jump out of her clothes. You'd better hurry."

"I'll wait till she jumps. Is she young and beautiful?"

"She is young and beautiful," Lucy said frostily, "and she is very scared, and I don't blame her. If you don't want somebody else to be murdered, you'd better get on over here. Because she's got one of those little dolls too."

4

Shayne left the phone booth and went out to his car, driving west as fast as the law allowed, pondering the circumstances which had brought two frightened people to his office today with voodoo dolls. Was this a new fad, like chain letters?

He discarded the idea distastefully as he recalled the graying face of Henny Henlein. The taking of human life, even a depraved life like Henlein's, wasn't to be regarded lightly.

It was a little after six when he strode into the anteroom of his third-floor office where Lucy sat typing. Through the partially opened door into the next room he could see a woman sitting in the chair beside his desk.

Lucy looked up reproachfully.

"Don't frown, angel. It makes wrinkles."

"Then hurry up," she whispered. "That woman's half crazy. I put her in your office because it made me jittery just to look at her."

"Who is she?"

"Somebody named Clarissa Milford. *Mrs.* Clarissa Milford."

"And you say she got one of the voodoo dolls?"

Lucy nodded.

Shayne looked through the door again. "She's quite a doll herself."

"She was when she came in. Waiting for you has aged her."

Shayne grinned and roughed her hair playfully with a big hand as he walked past her to his office.

He closed the door only partially and looked at Clarissa Milford. Lucy hadn't exaggerated. This was about the most upset woman he had ever seen. When she left home she had probably looked neat—she was wearing a trim blue suit with a ruff of white lace at her throat and she carried white gloves. But since then she had apparently been pulling at herself. Wisps of honey-blond hair hung from the bun at her neck. Her lipstick, except for a thin rim at the outer edge, had been eaten off. The red nail polish on all but the last two fingers of her left hand was flaked unevenly, and she was chewing on one of them when he came in. She wore a plain gold wedding ring.

She looked up at Shayne with a kind of wild expectancy. She had a small, straight nose, clear blue eyes and creamy skin. When she was not under strain, she must have had the statuesque chic of a model.

"Relax, Mrs. Milford." Shayne walked over to his desk. "We won't get anywhere until you do."

She folded her hands tightly in her lap. "I'll try." Her voice was tense. "But things have been happening so fast. Only last week my nephew, Jimsey Thain, was killed by a hit-and-run driver."

The words came out in a rush. "He was only twelve," she continued breathlessly, "and he was close to us—like our own. It was my car that killed him." She swallowed hard and reached in her purse for a handkerchief. Her hand was trembling.

"Your car?" he repeated incredulously.

"Oh, I didn't do it. I wasn't driving. My car had been parked in front and I never left the house. It must have been stolen—by teenagers maybe."

"What makes you say that?"

"I don't know. I shouldn't have. Everyone blames everything on teenagers these days. It could have been anybody, I guess. The car was found abandoned just a short way from where Jimsey's body was found. You must have read about it in the papers. It was only last week—"

"Nobody saw the accident?"

"No. The section isn't heavily settled. Whoever did it could have walked away easily without being seen."

"Mrs. Milford," Shayne said gently, "this isn't really what you came to see me about, is it?"

"No." She waited to get her voice under control. "On top of everything else, this morning I got this." She opened her purse again, took out a small doll and laid it carefully on a corner of the desk.

The redhead picked it up. It was identical to the ones Henlein had shown him a few hours earlier and, like one of them, had a black-headed pin protruding from its chest.

He laid it down, wrinkled his heavy red brows and tugged his left earlobe. What possible connection could there be between a small-time gangster and this extraordinarily pretty housewife? Could two people with such widely separated backgrounds have a common enemy? It did not, on the surface, seem reasonable. Yet the fact that Henny Henlein had been killed after receiving the dolls took this case out of the realm of fantasy and reasonless fear and put it starkly in the world of reality where fear was justified.

There was one difference between this doll and the ones Henlein had received. Glued to the black yarn hair was a yellow strand which might have come from Mrs. Milford's own head.

"Do you think this is yours?" He fingered the hair.

"No. The texture's different and it's straight. Mine has a slight wave when it's not pulled tight. And the color's a little off. Look." She picked up the doll and held it next to her head. The yellow strand was noticeably lighter and did not have the same golden tinge.

"Then we don't have to start figuring who might have had an opportunity to get a strand of your hair." Shayne leaned back in his swivel chair, took a pack of cigarettes from his pocket and extended it to her.

He lit both hers and his own, then asked, "Do you think someone believes *you* ran over your nephew, and sent you the doll to frighten you?"

She shuddered. "I don't know. I don't think so. No, I don't see why anyone would think that."

"How was the doll sent?"

"It wasn't. It was left. On the kitchen table while I was out. We live in the country and seldom lock our doors."

"You have no neighbors?"

"Only my sister and brother-in-law, Mabel and Percy Thain, Jimsey's parents. They live in a house that's a twin to ours about an acre away. But they were out too. The same place my husband and I were."

"Where was that?"

She hesitated, seeming a little embarrassed. "At a seance."

"At Madame Swoboda's?"

"Yes." She puffed at her cigarette nervously. "How did you know?"

"It's the one getting the best play right now. Do you attend many seances, Mrs. Milford?"

"Yes," she said slowly. "It's not that I believe in them—though I suppose I do a little or why would I be so terrified at having received the doll?"

Recalling what had happened to Henny Henlein, Shayne knew she had reason to be afraid.

"I guess it's the idea," she continued unsteadily, "that someone *wants* to kill me that upsets me. That anyone could hate me that much."

"It would upset anyone. Now think hard. Do you have any idea who might want to kill you?"

Shayne had expected a bewildered and positive denial. He was surprised when she said, "Yes."

"Who is it?"

"It might be—Madame Swoboda."

"Why should she want to kill you?"

"Maybe she doesn't. Maybe she's only trying to frighten me. But she does hate me."

"Why? And why do you attend her seances then?"

"Because of my husband," she said sadly. "Because he wants me to—or did at first. Dan's always been interested in the occult. And he's superstitious, like all gamblers."

"Is that his profession—gambling?"

"Oh, no. He's a real-estate broker. Gambling is his—hobby, he calls it."

"You don't call it that?"

"I call it a disease! Lately he's been burning 'success candles' that he gets from Madame Swoboda—the pink ones." She leaned forward, snuffing out her cigarette in an ash tray with unnecessary violence. "But Dan isn't the only reason I've been going to the seances. Since their son was killed, my sister, Mabel, and her husband have been going to Madame Swoboda's, too—in the hope of talking to Jimsey."

"And have they?"

Clarissa smiled wryly, the first change her face had shown. "They think they have. There's a voice. It doesn't sound much like Jimsey's to me, but Madame Swoboda would claim that's because of the cosmic distance it has to travel. The voice says characterless things like, 'I miss you Mommy and Daddy, but I'm happy here.' And garbled things that start out as if they're going to be important, but that never quite come off. There's nothing to prove it's Jimsey. He doesn't answer questions. After a few sentences he'll say he's tired from break-

51

ing through and wants to go back. That sort of thing."

She paused, clenching her hands again tightly in her lap. "It outrages me to see them so taken in."

Shayne rubbed his lean jaw and turned his eyes to the window for a moment. "Still, even if your husband and your sister and her husband go, why do you have to, if you believe Madame Swoboda is a fake? And especially if you suspect that she sent you the doll? Incidentally, you haven't told me yet why you think she might want to—at least—frighten you."

Tears welled suddenly in the woman's eyes and she seemed, in that instant, unable to move. She let them form and roll down her cheeks before she brought up the handkerchief to wipe them away. "I'm losing my husband," she said in a barely audible voice. "I thought at first that if I did what Dan wanted, if I attended the seances and tried to see things his way, it would give us a mutual interest that might bring us close again. Now—" she swallowed hard to quell the rising sob— "I think he's in love with Madame Swoboda."

"In love with Madame Swoboda?" Shayne's incredulous eyes rested on the classic loveliness of Clarissa's face.

"Yes. She isn't what you think, Mr. Shayne. Madame Swoboda is no raggle-tag gypsy. I don't know what her real name is, but she's young— younger than I am—and devastating, from a male point of view. I've watched Dan look at her, and other men too. She's beautiful and cool, but there's fire underneath. She's not spiritual, she's earthy. And she's soulless!"

"She sounds dangerous," Shayne murmured appreciatively. "Did your husband tell you he was in love with her?"

"No, but he's asked for a divorce." She fell silent, then said, "I wouldn't—I couldn't!—give it to him. I love him too much."

"Might he have left you the doll?"

Clarissa raised one pale hand uncertainly to push a wisp of gold hair back into the bun. "I don't know. Dan believes in black magic himself to some extent. He's like a child that way. That's why, at first, I didn't want to come to see you. I think I was afraid of what you might find out. You see, Mr. Shayne, I'm heavily insured." Her voice trailed off.

"Assume for the moment that Swoboda left you the doll. Why did she? To frighten you off so she can marry your husband? Is she in love with him? Could she profit financially or any other way by marrying him?"

"I don't see how she could profit in any other way, and I don't know if she is in love with him or not. I only sense how Dan feels about her. But Madame Swoboda hates me for another reason that has nothing to do with Dan. I was concerned about Mabel, my sister—she's been so terribly upset since Jimsey was killed and so has Percy—and I didn't want them to live on the false hope they get from seances. The strain is awful and I was afraid they might crack up. So I went to Madame Swoboda the other day and accused her of being a fraud and capitalizing on people's tragedies and fears, and I threatened to turn her over to the police." Clarissa paused thoughtfully. "It was curious. My threat seemed to frighten her more than I expected it would."

"She didn't agree to stop the seances, though."

"No. She refused to accept any responsibility for Mabel or Percy or any of her *clients*, I guess you'd call them. She insisted that it was the spirits who spoke through her, and she was only the host, the medium through which they spoke. And then I made a beaut of a mistake. I said the spirits spoke to me, too, and they told me she was trying to steal my husband. I said she'd never do it, except over my dead body.

"She said, 'It would be a pleasure that way!' So you see, if she didn't already have the idea of getting Dan away from me, I gave it to her."

Clarissa fumbled unsteadily in her purse, took out a pack of cigarettes and offered one to Shayne, waiting until he had lit them both before she added, "The worst of it is that now I'm so jealous I can't bear to let Dan go to the seances alone. So I'll have to face her again."

"Tonight?"

Clarissa nodded and, for the first time, allowed anger to creep into her voice. "It outrages me to see her victimize Mabel and Percy, but they refuse to miss a night. That's another reason I go. If she plays too much on their emotions, if they break down or go to pieces, I want to be there to help them."

54

"I understand. Now, let's go back to something you said a minute ago. When you threatened to turn Swoboda over to the police you say she seemed frightened."

"Yes. She laughed, but it was a nervous laugh—too loud and too long. Then she began to defend herself. She said she was operating scrupulously within the law. She was an entertainer, nothing more. I thought she protested too much."

"She might have a criminal record," Shayne said. "I'll check on it."

"Then you will take the case?"

"I'll take it." He smiled reassuringly. "I'll be at the seance tonight too. What time does it start?"

"At eight. But you have to be there at a quarter of. They won't let you in after it starts."

"That doesn't leave me much time, but I'll make it—with a reporter from the *News*. We'll blow this thing wide open."

She looked up gratefully, her eyes warm. "I'm glad I came to you. It was for myself at first—I wanted to find out who sent the doll because I was afraid—but if you can help Mabel and Percy too by exposing this criminal fraud . . ." Her voice trailed off into a little sigh of weariness.

"A last question before you go, Mrs. Milford." From the first, the circumstances of two such dissimilar people as Henny Henlein and Clarissa Milford receiving the voodoo dolls had intrigued Shayne. "Does the name Henry Henlein mean anything to you?"

She thought a moment and said, "No."

"Or *Henny* Henlein? He's a local hoodlum, or was."

"I'm sure I never heard of him."

"What about De Luca—sometimes called by his initials, D. L.?"

"You mean the gangster? I've seen his name in the papers, that's all."

Shayne rose and looked down on Clarissa Milford's smooth golden head. She was tall, but her bones were light and her waist was small and she gave the impression of delicate fragility. He moved his glance down, past breasts which made a firm thrust against the thin fabric of her blouse, to legs which could have modeled for a stocking ad, then returned to her face again. She was putting on lipstick, her blue eyes focused intently on the tiny vanity mirror. When she snapped it shut and looked up at him she seemed to be one of those rare feminine creatures without imperfection.

"Why should a woman as wholly lovely as you stick to a man who's fool enough not to want her?" he asked impulsively.

The beginning smile left her lips. "I know I should have more pride, but it's something I can't help. I guess I'm a one-man woman, or abnormally possessive, or maybe just plain selfish. You know women like that, don't you?"

"I do, but I don't think you're one of them."

"I'm afraid I am. I have a strong streak of jealousy. It runs all through our family. My sister, Mabel, and I, and my mother and father—we were all jealous of each other at times. But, as far as Dan goes, I married him because I loved him, and no matter what he does or how little he cares for me, I can't stop loving him. I know I can't. I've tried."

"Well, it's nothing to be ashamed of." Shayne's gray eyes were gentle. "Though it does seem a waste."

"No," she said vehemently. "No, it isn't. I know Dan's good! And somehow I can't really believe he doesn't love me still. Or maybe it's only that I can't accept it," she finished sadly.

Shayne patted her arm and walked with her through the outer office. She smiled at him softly before the door closed behind her.

Lucy swung around in her chair, looking up at the redhead with hard, brown eyes. "May I ask you a question, Michael Shayne?"

"Sure, angel. Shoot."

"Why should a woman as wholly lovely as I am stick to a man who regards her only as a piece of office equipment?"

Shayne grinned crookedly. "Because you love him, eavesdropper."

"I do not love you and I was not eavesdropping! You purposely left the door open so I could hear you."

"You misjudge me, Lucy. And besides, this enterprise holds you in higher esteem than it does a piece of office equipment."

"This enterprise!" She sniffed.

Shayne leaned over her desk and bent to rest his cheek on her silky brown hair. "I'm sorry, angel. I was planning on a little extra-office activity tonight, starting with dinner at Luigi's, but this other woman came along."

"That wholly lovely one? And you liked her better?"

"Impossible. But she needs me more. Being needed is very important to a man."

"To a woman, too." Lucy sighed. "Imagine having a man all to one's self. A man who wasn't pulled in six directions at once."

"That's pure selfish imagining. Anyway, I'm not pulled in six directions. Only yours and Clarissa's. And if I had my choice, I'd take yours."

5

"Get Bill Martin on the phone, please, angel," Shayne said.

"The private detective?" Lucy asked incredulously. "He's your competition."

"I resent that. He's a rank newcomer, just hung out his shingle. I'm not even sure he can handle a tailing job."

Lucy riffled through the phone book indignantly. "I get the complete picture now. Two people brought you voodoo dolls today. In fact, Mr. Henlein brought you two. But you wouldn't even give him time to tell you about them—just hustled him out to be killed. However, when a pretty woman— a wholly lovely one—comes in with only one doll, you turn over heaven and earth to protect her." She dialed the number with unnecessary vigor and handed the receiver to Shayne.

"You're not being logical, Lucy."

"That wasn't a requirement when you hired me."

"It's just because Henlein *was* murdered," Shayne said evenly, "that I'm getting someone to keep an eye on Clarissa Milford. And I'm not turning over heaven and earth to do it. I'm merely hiring Bill Martin who, as I said, doesn't rate very high in the profession anyway."

He stopped and spoke into the phone. "Hello, Bill? This is Shayne. I'd like you to do a little job for me—if you have time."

"I've got plenty." Martin had a boyish voice, too placating, too enthusiastic. "That is," he amended, "I'm pretty rushed, but I'll do it for you, Mike. What is it?"

"Protection. Around the clock—until further notice. And you'd better carry a gun." Shayne held out his hand for the piece of paper Lucy, the perfect secretary, had anticipated he'd want, and read into the phone an address in the remote northeast section of the city. "Better start now. She'll be getting home soon."

"Righto, Mike. Until further notice. Thanks, Mike." Typical of a young comer, he mentioned Shayne's first name too often.

The redhead hung up and reached for his hat. "Call Tim Rourke and ask him to meet me at Swoboda's at exactly quarter to eight tonight. And, angel—" He ran a hand thoughtfully over his lean jaw—"Tim was telling me the other day about a transistor recorder, pocket size. I don't remember the trade name, but he'll know what you mean. It's a new import from West Germany. Tell him to come loaded with that."

Lucy nodded, then said, "Take me, Michael. I've heard so much about Madame Swoboda."

60

"Sorry." Shayne shook his head. "Two women are all I can handle tonight."

"Two?"

"The Madame and Clarissa. But don't look so hurt. Maybe I'll take you next time. How do I know it's a fit place until I look it over?"

"Don't think I'll buy that, Michael Shayne! After all the joints you've lugged me in and out of—"

"Can't risk it any more. You're too good a secretary." He grinned, bent down and pressed a firm kiss on the bridge of her nose, directly between her eyes. At the door he turned. "Why don't you take in a movie?"

"Maybe I will. And a new gentleman friend too."

Shayne stopped at The Angus, grabbed a quick meal of rare steak and brandy, got into his car and turned toward the Miami River and Southwest Sixth Avenue.

At a little before quarter to eight, he drew up in front of a ramshackle house that had once been painted yellow. One side was propped on stilts precariously bedded in the Miami River, the roof shingles were damp and mildewed, and the stone sidewalk leading from the curb to a small railed porch was muddy and, in places, gave under his weight as he walked up to the door.

Several cars, some with out-of-state licenses, were parked in front and across the street. Among them he recognized Rourke's beat-up coupé. Yet from outside there was little evidence that the house held visitors. Except for a dim bulb in the front hall and a diffused green glow coming from beneath one of the drawn drapes, no light showed.

Shayne paused for a moment on the small porch, his nostrils flaring, trying to place a sweet, indefinable odor. The front door was of heavy pine, with a stained glass transom through which light from a yellow bulb shone.

A small card above the bell read *Walk in* in letters crudely penned with black ink. Shayne turned the handle of the door and opened it. Inside, the odor was stronger.

On the right of a small entrance hall was a sliding door, tightly closed. On the other side an open arch was half-blocked by a desk behind which a middle-aged woman wearing brown, horn-rimmed glasses sat guard over a green cash box and a pad and pencil. Over the pad stood another crudely inked card, saying *Messages.*

"To the other world?" Shayne nodded toward the card.

"To the departed," the woman affirmed in a voice as unctuous as an undertaker's. "If this is your first time here I'd better tell you that we allow few questions—inside." The faint pause before the last word and the drop in her voice gave full and relevant value to it. However, the reverence with which she pronounced the next words, "That'll be five dollars," took away some of the effect.

Dropping a five on the desk, the redhead walked past her into the next room. It was furnished like a doctor's waiting room except that there were no magazines. The furniture consisted of benches on which three people might sit with only small discomfort, and straight wooden chairs. A round pine table in the center was bare except for an incense burner from which the sickening odor of sandalwood emanated. The only light came from a green-shaded lamp.

Shayne spotted Tim Rourke seated alone on a bench, bent over, his lean legs widely separated. His thin hands twirled his hat between his legs while he stared at the floor. Shayne's eye flicked past the baggy coat pocket where the recorder might well be concealed, to Tim's belt buckle which doubled for a crystal microphone.

On another bench Clarissa Milford sat, wedged between a man and a woman, probably her sister and brother-in-law, for the man wore a black mourning band on one sleeve. Clarissa gave him a faint nod of negation, and Shayne walked past her without speaking and sat down beside Tim Rourke.

The reporter's emaciated face stretched into the thin smile he might give a stranger; he nodded slightly and went back to twirling his hat.

Putting a cigarette to his lips, Shayne spoke behind his hand in a barely audible voice and without looking at Tim. "You set with the pick-up?"

"Yeah." Rourke's lips hardly moved. "What you want taped?"

"The whole seance."

Rourke nodded and Shayne fell silent. Where, he wondered, was Clarissa Milford's husband? Since Dan Milford was the one who really believed in the seances, it was a little curious that tonight he should not be here. In the weighted silence, he studied Clarissa's benchmates.

Her sister, Mabel, sat stiffly as if she were so tightly corseted that her spine was held rigid. Her shoulders were square and her wrists, where they showed below the sleeves of her black dress, were thin and bony. Her brown, straight hair was pulled back severely into a bun—not the chic bun Clarissa wore, but an old-fashioned braided twist. Had it not been for a formation of bone around the eyes and a fleeting expression at the mouth, Shayne would have found it hard to believe that the two could be sisters.

The man with the mourning band on the sleeve of his light gray suit looked shorter than Mabel. Except for the grim set of his mouth, Percy Thain would have been innocuous looking, but bereavement, rage and rebellion against the tragic death of his son were apparent in his face and in the bleak lifelessness of his eyes.

At ten minutes to eight two other couples entered —tourists, judging from their spruce vacation clothing—and, in their wake, another couple. Shayne's knobby fingers massaged his left earlobe.

The man was the balding, angel-haloed man called Ed whom he had met on Sylvester's boat that afternoon. His wife was about what Shayne would have expected; middle-aged and showing it, dumpy but trying to conceal it with tight corsets and high heels.

Above the white sport shirt Ed's face loomed raw

and burned. The fringe of hair was smoothed and stuck down with water, and he was chewing a thick cigar, perhaps one the Cuban had dropped on the *Santa Clara* as an afterthought. The belt holding his trousers circled below his pot-belly obscenely, but his suit was made of soft flannel and looked expensive.

Ed glanced casually around the dimly-lit room, doing a slight double-take when his eyes met Shayne's. He nodded curtly and led his wife to one of the hard-backed benches.

It was hard to believe this granite-visaged man and the jovial, drunken Ed on the boat this afternoon were the same, and hard to conceive of Ed's being interested in the occult. His wife might have forced him to come, but in spite of his wry claim this afternoon that his wife made him clean the fish he caught, he didn't seem like a man a wife could dominate.

Three other tourists, all women, entered, gave everyone the stranger's smile and sat down. Apparently in this society neither conversation nor introductions were in order. And curiously, though the out-of-towners were almost certainly in Miami on vacation and at Madame Swoboda's only for amusement there was no laughing or talking. It might be the atmosphere, or the fact that they were about to explore, however shallowly, something they did not understand, which cast a pall of solemnity over them.

Another couple entered, and finally a lone woman, thin-faced and gray, clutching a large black bag. She, like the Thains and Clarissa Milford, looked like a regular. There was nothing of the vacationer about her.

At two minutes to eight the woman in the horn-rimmed glasses picked up the cash box and walked down the hall. In less than a minute she was back, standing in the doorway.

"You may come in now." Her voice was rarefied. She stepped across the small hallway as the crowd rose, opened a pair of sliding doors and held a heavy black velvet curtain aside to allow them to file in.

Except for a pale green light emanating from a round ball, the room was dark. At the far end of a large oval table, the dim form of Madame Swoboda sat, erect in an armless chair, hands flat on the table in front of her, one on either side of the green ball. The light shone up eerily into her face, emphasizing the caverns of her eyes and her high cheekbones. Her large, black-lashed eyes were open, fastened unblinkingly on a distant point ahead. She seemed already in a trance, unaware that anyone had entered.

She wore a silver shawl crossed over her bosom, which emphasized her full breasts, and a tiara-like circle on her ebony hair from which silver gossamer material fell in soft folds to her waist. Her features were regular, her skin clear and fair, her face beautiful and tantalizing. Yet underneath, despite her apparent removal from the world of reality, there was that fire Clarissa Milford had described. She was vital and earthy.

Behind her was a closed, unadorned cabinet between windows draped, like the sliding doors, from ceiling to floor in heavy black velvet. No sliver of light came through.

She remained motionless as they felt their way around the table, pulled out chairs and sat down. Shayne managed to sit beside Ed, his fishing companion of the afternoon. Mabel Thain was on the other side.

When quiet had settled, Madame Swoboda spoke, her voice weirdly monotonous in the dark: "Once more we journey . . . together we reach out . . . in unison we call . . ." The timbre of her voice was deep, intriguing, sexy, with only a faint, indefinable suggestion of a foreign accent.

"For those new among us . . . link your own thumbs. Link the little finger on each hand with that of the person beside you. The circle travels, never ending. . . . Wait . . . wait . . . wait. The dead are inarticulate."

There was a faint rustling as they found each other's hands. Then a deep quiet settled in. Shayne was aware of Ed's slightly damp fat finger on his right, and Mabel Thain's thin, dry one on his left.

Again Madame Swoboda spoke. "For the success of our journey I repeat, three times, the Ninety-eighth Psalm: *He hath done marvelous things. His right hand and His holy arms hath gotten Him the victory. . . . He hath done marvelous things. His right hand and His holy arms hath gotten Him the victory. . . . He hath done marvelous things. His right hand and His holy arms hath gotten Him the victory. . . .*"

Silence crept in again, silence with a weighted, brooding quality. It might have been phony as a district attorney's pity, except that forces reaching out from this dark room had, in some way and to some degree, been responsible for the death of one person today and were threatening at least one other.

The dim light shone up into Madame Swoboda's still face. She had closed her eyes, the long lashes resting sootily against the white cheeks. As Shayne watched, she shivered violently once and then was quiet. The circle at the table held.

After a time she said, "I have sent your messages."

Another silence. The room was filled with breathing. Finally, from somewhere high in the room a man's voice sounded. It had a curiously metallic quality: "Sharon . . . I am here. I have your message. . . . My marriage was a mistake. It was you I loved and wanted. . . ."

A woman's voice came next through the darkness, softly and incoherently, describing the Great Beyond. She addressed a man called Bill. After her, came another voice tiredly reiterating, "I am happy," and addressing no one.

At last, a child's thin voice sounded, first far away, then coming closer. "Mother . . . Daddy. . . . At last I have gotten through to you. It is so far. For two hours and thirty-six minutes I have traveled . . . through the forty-eight outer worlds . . ."

Mabel Thain breathed, "It's Jimsey!" and tightened her grip on Shayne's finger.

On his right, Ed stirred restlessly, the grip of his

little finger loosening, then tightening. What, Shayne wondered again, could be the attraction here for this man who seemed to be only a pleasure-bent tourist? If he had come to please his wife, or only for casual amusement, why the tension? On the other hand, what kind of mystically inclined person drank hundred-and-fifty proof rum, drooled idiotically at a girl doing a hooch dance on a Cuban boat and put a dirtied-up, souped-up engine in Sylvester's fishing boat?

The child's voice continued: "I am well . . . and happy . . . but when I lay dying Friday night, I spoke your name eight times . . ." A blue light wavered across the ceiling, then disappeared. "Mother . . . Daddy . . . Good-by."

Madame Swoboda sighed, sat quietly for a long moment as though all strength had left her, then shivered and opened her eyes.

"That is all." Her voice had a deep, unworldly timbre. "The spirits are tired. The seance is over."

She rose quickly, passed through the sliding doors, walked down the hall and disappeared. The lights went on, two dim yellow bulbs in a wall fixture. Everyone blinked against the sudden light, released each other's fingers a little sheepishly, scraped back their chairs and got to their feet. Shayne looked at Ed. His lips were moving sound-lessly, his brows knit in concentration.

Ed rose finally and pushed through the low-voiced crowd to reach his wife at the other side of the table. Shayne caught Tim Rourke's cynical eye, then moved between the stragglers to intercept Ed and his wife, who were pushing with the others to the door.

Clapping Ed on the back, the redhead said, "So we meet again. You never can tell where a tourist will turn up in this town."

"Or a detective," Ed retorted. Turning to his wife, he said, "Dear, this is the detective I was telling you about who was on the boat today. Mike Shayne. Mike, meet the wife."

"It's a pleasure, Mrs.—"

"Woodbine." She poked Ed playfully. "Didn't you even tell Mr. Shayne your last name?"

"We were all on a first name basis," Shayne said. "It was only by accident that Sylvester happened to mention *my* name. Where are you folks staying?"

A quick glance passed between the man and woman, then Ed said openly, "Blue Grotto Hotel. Know it?"

"Very well."

"At one of the cabanas," Mrs. Woodbine said. "Number sixteen. Come and see us, Mr. Shayne."

"Maybe I will. Thanks. How did you enjoy the seance?"

She shrugged matronly shoulders. "It's something to do—I get so tired of canasta—but I don't think I can ever drag Ed here again. He was bored stiff."

Shayne said, "Maybe if you feed him bonito again it'll put him in the mood."

"Bonito?" She looked genuinely puzzled.

"I started to bring a fish home, honey," Ed explained, "but I couldn't face cleaning it, so I gave it away."

She sighed in exasperation. "You fish all day and then give away what you catch! It makes more sense to play canasta."

Ed shrugged and winked, probably thinking of the Demerara he had consumed that afternoon, then took his wife firmly by the arm and faced her toward the door, asking, a little brusquely, "What are *you* doing here, Mike? Casing the joint?"

"You might call it that."

"As far as I can see, it's harmless. I don't go for this out-of-the-world stuff, but the Madame puts on a good show. If this is what they want, they get their money's worth." He propelled his wife to the door.

The desk in the arch next to the waiting room was now covered with voodoo dolls, boxes of pink, red, black and white candles, labeled *Success, Love, Death* and *Immortality,* small bottles holding *Goofer Dust,* amulets attached to bracelets and necklaces, and a stack of occult literature. People were crowding around the desk to buy souvenirs from the woman in the horn-rimmed glasses. The prices, Shayne noted, were not exorbitant.

At a touch on his arm, he turned.

"Mr. Shayne, someone has been following me." Clarissa Milford stood behind him, her eyes wide and disturbed.

"I know. I hired him."

"Then you must think I'm in danger!" she whispered.

"It's only a precaution." Shayne picked up one of the voodoo dolls and dropped a half dollar on the desk. Even without comparing this doll closely to the ones Henny Henlein and Clarissa Milford had gotten, he could tell they were all from the same lot.

"I'd like you to meet my sister and brother-in-law, Mr. and Mrs. Thain," Clarissa said with a complete change of voice. "This is Michael Shayne."

Shayne nodded to Mabel, took Thain's limp hand and looked down into brown, hostile eyes.

"The detective?" Thain turned to Clarissa. "What have you to do with him?"

"Oh, you know, Percy," Clarissa said offhandedly. "It's about that doll."

"I see," Thain said distantly. "I didn't know you had gone to him."

"I decided suddenly—"

"If it makes her feel better, Percy—" Mabel said placatingly.

Relations between the Thains and Clarissa seemed a trifle strained. Did Percy Thain believe Clarissa to be more involved in the hit-and-run death of his son than she admitted? And was she?

The Thains left with Clarissa, and Tim Rourke walked over. The sensation-seekers had thinned out, most of them gone. "I'm afraid we wasted our time," Rourke said. "There's no story here."

Shayne ran a hand over his angular jaw. "I'm not so sure. You think it came through O.K. on your pocket recorder?"

"Such as it is, I've got it."

"I'd like to run it through a little later and listen again."

"What for?" Rourke asked sourly. "It's gobbledegook. By the way, Sharon, the person the first message was addressed to, was that thin woman. I was sitting next to her. She shook like a leaf."

"She must be a regular. Otherwise the tape couldn't have been prepared."

"It was about the only message that made sense."

"Maybe," the redhead said slowly, "the others made sense to someone."

"What do you mean? All that gabble about the forty-eight outer worlds couldn't make sense to anyone except another ectoplasm. Maybe you don't get around in occult circles, Mike. It's old hat. This kind of thing's done every day. If it were a con game— But I don't see any racket angle. The Madame puts on a good show and folks get their money's worth."

It was the same thing Ed Woodbine had emphasized, and precisely what Shayne himself was thinking. "They got more than their money's worth. That's what bothers me. At five dollars a performance and fifty cents a doll, she's damn near losing money."

Rourke scratched his head. "You think it's set up as a front for something? Could be. But I don't see what."

"I don't either. But I've had two frightened clients today with dolls that came from here, and one was murdered this afternoon."

"You talking about Henny Henlein? You've been holding out on me, Mike."

"I'll give it to you as soon as it can be printed."

Rourke looked at Shayne through narrowed eyes.

73

"Are the dolls the only thing that's worrying you?"

"No. There was a man here I'm curious about. I met him this afternoon on Sylvester's boat. He's a vacationist—but not the type I'd figure to shoot a tropical evening at Madame Swoboda's."

"Hell, Mike, I think you're straining. People do things when they get to Miami they'd never think of doing anywhere else. Maybe the sun gets them. Or maybe they just get tired of fishing and an ectoplasmic evening seems like a good change. Or maybe they get tired of communing with their wives and decide to give the spirits a whirl."

"I'd rather whirl a real body—even if it was my wife."

"So would I," Rourke said. "Especially if it was your wife."

Shayne grinned. "Speaking of that, I think I'll go and find out what Swoboda's like without her astral body."

"I'll run along then. Want me to burn a pink *Success* candle for you?"

"I'm sure it's not necessary," Shayne said.

6

The redhead walked down the hall past the seance room in the direction Madame Swoboda had taken. The hall ended at a kitchen, off which a narrow stairway led upstairs. He mounted the steps, purposely making his footsteps heavy, and found at the top another narrow hallway, dimly lit, and leading to the front of the house.

The first room he passed was an old-fashioned bath with a footed tub and a box over the toilet with a long chain dangling from it. The second was a bedroom, sparsely furnished and uninviting, and the third, a sort of den in which Madame Swoboda was sitting in a wicker rocker.

The gossamer veiling and tiara lay on the floor beside her, but she still wore the silver shawl crossed over her ample and worldly breasts. The lamplight brought out the red lights in her black hair and emphasized the extraordinary length of her lashes. A highball stood on a battered victorian table at her elbow, and smoke wafted upward from the cigarette she held between slim fingers.

She turned, startled, as Shayne entered, asking coldly, "What do you want here?"

"To tell you how impressive you were." Shayne toed a chair around to face her and sat down in it.

Accepting the compliment, she said, "I have the gift. I'm a born medium." Picking up the drink she took a deep draught, then set it down and puffed on the cigarette.

"Are you the deep-trance type?" The redhead was amused at the contrast between hard liquor, tobacco and the spiritual claim. "Or are you semi-trance?"

"Deep," she said in her timbred voice. She fastened enormous gray eyes on him, the black lashes spreading around them like spider legs. They looked bottomless, seeming to hold slumbering fire, feminine provocation and worldly knowledge—everything, in fact, but spiritual light. "In a trance I feel exhilarated, I feel profound, but—" she sighed heavily—"it is tiring. I need stimulation after it is over."

Shayne grinned and abandoned the rarity he had been putting into his voice. "I understand. I'm not exactly a teetotaler myself."

"Don't I know you from somewhere?" Her eyes narrowed.

"I don't think so. How long have you been in this business?"

"That's none of yours!"

"I'd like it to be," Shayne said softly.

She looked at him speculatively, some of the hardness melting. "Why?"

"Beautiful women are a hobby with me."

She smiled slowly, showing white, even teeth, let the smile die and raised her eyebrows aloofly. "Hobbies don't interest me—particularly other people's."

"Who are you?"

"Kyra Swoboda."

"Nuts! Who were you before. Jenny Hopfstedder? Mary Murphy?"

"To you," she said coldly, "I'm Madame Swoboda. And I think it's time you were getting the hell out of here."

Shayne rose, moved in front of her and rested one hand on each arm of her chair, completely fencing her in. She looked up provocatively, eyes quizzical and inviting, her moist lips slightly parted so that the tips of her white teeth showed. A movement went through her body—a movement wholly material and physical. Looking down, Shayne saw the mounds of her breasts outlined by the crossed shawl. They rose and fell as her breathing quickened.

"You could be a career," Shayne said huskily.

"That interests me more."

He was bending to kiss her when her eyes quickened with recognition. She drew back, forcibly removed one of his hands from the chair arm and squeezed past him, rising and walking across the room with a lithe animal stride.

"I thought I recognized you when I first saw you out there this evening. Your picture's been in enough papers. You ought to start wearing a beard, Mr. Shayne."

"It's not becoming—"

"What do you want with me?" she asked harshly.

"Your background."

"Why?"

"Let's say it's a matter of close personal interest."

"That's not true!"

"All right then. I'm investigating a murder. A man was found dead today. His name was Henry Henlein and he had received two of your little dolls, one stabbed, one strangled."

She laughed humorlessly. "What have I to do with that? Hundreds of people have bought them. We don't keep records."

"You keep a record of those who attend your seances regularly. Otherwise you wouldn't be able to prepare the tape recordings in advance. Who does attend them regularly—besides the Thains and the Milfords?"

"I don't know. There are no tapes and I don't keep records!" There was venom in her voice.

"What about the Woodbines? Are they regulars?"

Her manner changed. She became softer, almost placating, as if she now wanted to co-operate. "I'm not sure who you mean."

"A chunky, bald-headed man, blond. His skin's peeling from sunburn. His wife's dumpy and middle-aged."

"It seems to me they've been here once or twice, but I'm not sure. Really," she smiled in sweet

78

reasonableness, "I hold a seance every night. Tourists come and go. I can't keep track of them all and don't try to. I have no reason to."

"What were you—before this?"

"I had a mentalist act. I was a mind-reader on the stage. Not that it's any of your business." She recovered her assurance suddenly, turned her back, jabbed her cigarette viciously in the ash tray and took another from a box on the table.

"Who set you up here?"

"I took my own money and set myself up. Now, will you get the hell out?"

"I hate to leave on this note. We were getting along so beautifully."

"We're not any more."

"One last question. Are you in love with Dan Milford?"

She swung around, her mouth set in a crimson line, her eyes flashing. "Now I get it! Now I know who sent you. Murder, indeed! It was that jealous wife of his! She came here, threatening to interfere with the way I make my living, throwing her weight around and upsetting me so I could hardly go into a trance that night."

She flipped the ashes of her cigarette irritably in the direction of an ash tray, then using it as a pointer, shook it at him.

Unaccountably, despite the show of anger and indignation, Shayne had a feeling that her true feeling at the moment was one of relief, almost as if she had welcomed mention of Dan Milford.

Ostensibly still holding to her anger, Swoboda said, "Whoever murdered that Milford woman would be doing a good deed."

"Is that why you sent her a voodoo doll—to scare her to death?"

She stopped, honestly surprised, her mouth agape, her aquiline nose uptilted, the flush of anger slowly receding. The respite was only temporary, however. On the next instant the fury returned.

"It's none of your damned business, but I didn't. Now, for the last time, get out! You're invading my privacy!"

"I'd like to. The idea's tempting. You're not going to answer my question about Dan Milford?"

"I am not." She threw herself into the wicker chair and rocked violently, staring sullenly ahead, the cigarette sending a wavy stream of smoke up from her moving hand.

Reaching out, Shayne touched her bare arm lightly with one finger.

She jumped. "What are you doing?"

"I wanted to see if you'd burn me. Dan Milford's wife says you're on fire."

"If I had my way, I would. The less Shaynes in this world, the better."

"And the more Swobodas?"

"What do you think, Shayne?"

"I don't know yet. Dan Milford's wife says you're soulless, too."

The moment of softness was gone. "Will you stop quoting that woman? And get out of here!"

80

"I'm on my way—but I'll be back. I think I'm a mystic, too."

She opened her mouth to release a flurry of abuse.

He ducked out fast.

7

When Shayne reached the street he found all the other cars gone except his own and a big gray sedan which he assumed belonged to Swoboda. It seemed a trifle incongruous for someone on familiar terms with the spirit world to be operating a contrivance as unethereal as a Buick, but of course even delvers into the occult had to get around some way, broomsticks being outdated in this age of rockets.

He opened the front door of his own car and slid behind the wheel. He had covered only a few blocks before he became aware that the gray Buick was behind him. The trenches in his lean face deepened, and he turned experimentally off Southeast Third Avenue, heading toward Biscayne Boulevard. The gray sedan turned too. He swung south, circled the block. The sedan followed.

No doubt about it, he'd picked up a tail.

He cruised slowly, his face bleak. He *could* play along with the tail and find out who it was—but that would take time.

Two pressing errands faced him. He wanted to see Clarissa Milford and the Thains and find out why, among other things, Dan Milford, who purported to take the seances so seriously, had stayed away tonight.

But even more compelling was the need for a clarifying talk with his little Cuban friend, Sylvester. Ed's presence at the seance was disturbing and the interview Shayne had just concluded with Swoboda had deepened his concern, for it was obvious that Swoboda had been on guard. She had sweet-talked when he brought Ed's name up and overacted her anger at mention of Clarissa and Dan Milford. The real object of her concern would seem to be the man from the fishing boat.

The fishing trip this afternoon had left him with a vague feeling of dissatisfaction, too, of things hinted at but not explained. Was it coincidence or connection which had caused a man from the boat to turn up at the seance? In any case, since murder unaccountably was breathing down the necks of some people, a talk with Sylvester was strongly indicated.

The redhead picked up speed, hit Biscayne and turned north. He found a corner that was police patrolled and when the yellow light flashed, sped through it and turned west at the next corner. Through the rear-view mirror he saw that the gray Buick had not made the light.

Still speeding, he turned south on Miami Avenue, circled back and headed toward the Causeway to

Miami Beach. Across the Causeway he turned south toward the slip where Sylvester's boat was docked.

The *Santa Clara* was there all right, squeaking gently against her rubber fenders in the slow swell of the water, but Sylvester wasn't. Shayne put a beam from his small pocket flash around the cabin, located the light switch and flicked it on. Everything looked shipshape. Sylvester must have slept off his overindulgence in Demerara rum, roused himself and gone home. It was a quick recovery and that was good. Maybe Sylvester wouldn't be as hung-over as he deserved.

On impulse the redhead opened the ice box. The big grouper he had caught this afternoon was still there. He slammed the door shut and prowled the cabin for a few minutes, looking at the charts, the cuddy and the gear compartment forward. There was nothing that didn't belong on a fishing boat and everything was in place.

Taking off the engine housing he probed with his flashlight at the new Gray Marine, dirtied up "to fool the tax collector," which had never been let out, Sylvester said. Still, the power was there if he needed it. Or if *they* needed it? Why would they need it? The three jolly vacationers *liked* Sylvester. That's the only reason they had bought him the new, very expensive engine for his boat. They had helped him to make a fast boat faster.

Leaving the *Santa Clara* Shayne slammed into his car and drove swiftly to a waterfront area, inhabited mostly by Cubans. He parked in front of a

84

two-story wooden tenement, went up two steps and pressed the bell button under the name that read *Sylvester Santos.*

A little, ample-bosomed, gray-haired woman wearing a pink-flowered housedress came to the door, her fleshy arms protruding from the short sleeves. Her face looked drawn, but her worried brown eyes kindled with pleasure when she recognized the redhead.

"Michael Shayne!" Her full lips spread in a welcoming smile and she stood aside. "Be so good to come in, Mr. Shayne."

Shayne walked into an apartment as neat and shipshape as Sylvester's boat, the woman following him, talking volubly.

"You look for my husband, no? Well, I tell you. He came home maybe one half hour ago, then go out again. To look for you, he say. But now you look for him. Mr. Shayne, what is the matter? These days I am most unhappy."

"Why does Sylvester look for me, Mrs. Santos?"

"He does not say. He says nothing to me but to talk of his new friends who are so good to him. But I do not like these new friends, Mr. Shayne. He is now drunk with them all the time and it is not like Sylvester to drink so much. Every day he comes home drunk and goes to bed dead. But tonight he comes home drunk and bleeding. One eye is black, and blood is on his face from fighting. I have to wipe it off and the cuts are deep. This is not like Sylvester, to fight—"

"Did he say he was in a fight?"

"No, but I can see he has been beaten and his clothes torn."

From the way Sylvester had been staggering around the deck this afternoon, his fight might have been only with the Demerara. Perhaps he had gotten up too quickly and fallen on his face a few times, or maybe he had been jackrolled on the way home. If that had happened it would explain why he had left home to look for his friend, "the detective who heads only the big cases."

"What does Sylvester say about his new friends?" Shayne asked.

She shrugged elaborately. "Only that they are so good to him. But I think they are drunk bums, Mr. Shayne, good only to get my husband drunk and in trouble and to spoil his health."

"May I use the phone, Mrs. Santos?"

"Sure. Help yourself. You're good man."

Shayne dialed and got his answering service. There had been no calls. Then he phoned Lucy and learned from her that Sylvester had not tried to reach him at her apartment either.

"How about a moonlight drive, angel?"

"Why, Michael, I'd love it," she said huskily. Suddenly, her voice changed. "Except that I know from past experience that your moonlit drives usually end up at some place like the morgue."

"Nothing like that tonight, Lucy. This will be sheer romance. I'll pick you up in ten minutes."

He hung up and walked back to Mrs. Santos, who had seated herself in an old-fashioned wooden rocker.

"Will you have Sylvester phone me when he comes in, no matter what time of night it is?"

"Sure, Mr. Shayne. Be glad to." She wiped her perspiring forehead with the back of her hand.

"And don't worry," he said. "Sylvester will be all right. Just like he was before, when these new friends go home."

"*Bueno*," she said. "I hope so."

Lucy was ready when Shayne rang her apartment bell. "Won't you come in, Michael?"

"Sorry, I can't, angel. Let's get going."

"Not even for a spot of Hennessy?"

"Not even for Hennessy. I'll take a brandy-check, though."

She closed the door and fell into step beside him. "What's the rush? Is the moon waning?"

"Time is. It's nearly midnight and I want to get out to Clarissa Milford's before she goes to bed."

"You're taking me with you to see another woman? I thought you said on the phone this was sheer romance."

"It is, for me. You're the chaperone."

"Oh, good! Just what I've always yearned to be."

As Shayne wheeled out from the curb, a gray sedan started up down the block.

Noticing how the redhead stared bleakly into the rear-view mirror, Lucy asked acutely, "Why should anyone tail you, Michael?"

"I don't know. Percy Thain found out at the seance that his sister-in-law, Clarissa, had hired me. He didn't like it much, but I don't think he could have rounded up a tail this fast. It was on me when

I left Swoboda's, but I ditched him. He must have staked out here on the chance that I'd see you."

"Then it's somebody who knows that I'm—your secretary, at least."

"At the very least." Shayne smiled a wry, warm smile.

"You don't seem worried."

"About your being—at least—my secretary, or about the tail?"

"About the tail, of course."

"I'm not. I'm not going anywhere tonight that I give a damn if anybody knows."

Lucy fell silent a moment, then said, in a small worried voice, "I don't see why it would be Percy Thain."

"I don't either. What's he got to gain by knowing where I go?"

"Nothing—unless he's the one who sent Clarissa Milford the voodoo doll. If he's really planning to kill her, he'd want to do it when you weren't around."

"Good figuring, but at this point I don't think it's Percy Thain. I can't figure what connection he'd have with a cheap hood like Henlein, and it's a good bet the same person sent dolls to both Clarissa and Henlein."

"Why?"

"Too much of a coincidence otherwise."

It was a moonless night and out in the country the dew was thick. The windshield clouded and Shayne started the wipers, listening to the rhythm of their faint, regular squeak as they swept across the glass.

After a while he slowed, turning his spot on the mailboxes. At the one reading Milford, he entered a long driveway.

A half a block in, the Milfords' house faced the Thains' across about an acre of untended ground. They were identical one-story, red-brick, L-shaped houses, with a small front stoop and detached garages, and they looked out of place so far from any other sign of community living. They sat in a deserted field, squat and ugly, combining city and country living in an almost comic way. While it wasn't difficult to picture Percy and Mabel Thain living out their lives within these lonesome, unimaginative walls, Clarissa Milford seemed out of place here. Perhaps she lived here because it was cheap. If her husband was a compulsive gambler, she'd need to keep a tight hand on the budget.

Across the way the Thains' house was dark, but a light shone behind drawn shades in the Milford living room.

As Shayne reached for the door handle, Lucy said, "I'll wait here for you, Michael."

"Just to prove you trust me with another woman?"

"No, but she's so upset. I think she'd rather talk to you alone."

"Angel." He slid across the seat and kissed her quickly. "You are a good angel. I won't be long."

As he walked across the thin sward of grass to

89

the front door and rang the bell, from the corner of his eye he caught a movement in a spotting of shrubbery. Bill Martin was on the job. It had probably been his light-colored convertible parked on the road.

Clarissa came to the door, wearing the same blue suit she had worn to the office this afternoon and at the seance. Her eyes were tight and she looked tired. When she recognized Shayne, fine lines appeared on her forehead.

"May I come in for a minute?"

"Of course." She stepped aside, a little reluctantly, adding, "My sister and brother-in-law are here."

"Maybe we could talk outside for a minute then."

She closed the door behind her, walked down the steps and out onto the sparse grass. About ten feet from the house she stopped, turned suddenly and said, "Dan hasn't come home yet. He called to say he was tied up—on business he said, but I know what kind. Have you found anything out yet?"

He smiled. "You've got to give me a little time. What do you mean—you know what kind of business your husband is tied up with tonight?"

She took the cigarette he offered and let him light it and then she said, "This afternoon I told you that Dan liked to gamble, but I—didn't tell you the whole thing. I guess I hoped I wouldn't have to. It doesn't have any bearing on what I came to see you about."

"Then why are you telling me now?"

"Because I think maybe you can help me. Dan's

in deep, Mr. Shayne. He's half-crazy with worry and and I am too—about him. Especially since he didn't come home tonight."

"Who does he owe the money to? Someone who won't wait?"

She nodded, looking down to avoid the redhead's eyes. "I wasn't quite honest with you this afternoon when I said the name De Luca didn't mean anything to me. He's the loan-shark Dan owes money to."

Shayne's interest quickened. He tapped the cigarette, sending sparks into the dark. Was this the connection between the pretty housewife and the dead hoodlum he had been looking for? Henlein had worked for De Luca, Dan Milford owed money to De Luca, and De Luca had been known to maim and kill men who failed to meet his usurious payments. Had one of De Luca's musclemen tried to get Dan Milford to pay up by leaving one of the voodoo dolls with his wife? It seemed an unlikely way for gangsters to operate—still, they had done more than frighten Henny Henlein, they had killed him.

There was another possibility. If Henny Henlein had been crowding Dan Milford for his loan-shark boss, De Luca, Dan might have killed Henlein.

"Does your husband know you got the doll?" Shayne asked abruptly.

"No. I didn't tell him."

"You told the Thains. Why didn't you tell him too? Unless you think he left it?"

She stared at him, her horror showing even in the

dark night. "If you knew him you'd never say that. Dan's not a murderer!"

"And you're not murdered—yet. But Henny Henlein is. Henlein was one of De Luca's muscle-men and collectors. Now that you've admitted you know De Luca, what do you know about Henlein?"

"Nothing. I was telling the truth about that. I never heard the name."

"You still haven't told me why you didn't tell your husband somebody left you the voodoo doll."

"I didn't want to worry him any more. He had enough to be worried about." She was crying softly. "And even if he *did* want to kill me—which he never would—why wouldn't he just do it, instead of sending me the doll?"

"You told me this afternoon he believed in the voodoo curse—that he was like a child that way."

"Dan would never hurt me, much less kill me. He wouldn't!"

"He wants to divorce you," Shayne said brutally. "He told you so. Maybe he's changed his mind about that and would like your insurance money instead. He'd be just as free to marry Madame Swoboda if you were dead as if you were divorced. And he'd be out from under De Luca's threat, with maybe some money left over."

"You're horrible, Mr. Shayne!" She whirled away from him and started toward the house.

He caught her arm and swung her around. She bumped against him and for a quick instant he felt her body warm and exciting against him. "You hired me to help you, Clarissa. That's what I'm trying to do."

She sobbed on his shoulder. "I know. I'm sorry to be making such a scene, but I'm so worried about Dan—"

"He's been out gambling before."

She drew away and wiped her eyes. "I don't think he's gambling tonight. I think he's trying to raise money to pay off D. L. And if he can't do it—and I don't know how he can—our house and car are mortgaged to the limit—I'm afraid of what D. L. will do. Dan may be beaten—or killed. Even now he may be dead—"

She stopped as light streamed from the just-opened door of the house.

"Clarissa!" Mabel called peremptorily. "Where are you?"

"Out here. Talking to Mr. Shayne."

"Good heavens, you've been at it long enough. And all over a silly doll somebody most likely left you for a joke. Well anyway, we're going home. Percy needs some sleep if he's going to work tomorrow."

"Don't go. I'm coming in now."

The Thains came down the steps anyway and moved toward them across the lawn.

"I wonder if you'd mind telling me," Shayne said as they came nearer, "how long you've been going to Madame Swoboda's?"

Mabel Thain stopped a few feet away. "Only since Jimsey's death," she said tightly. "Dan took us and we found it comforting."

"How long has Dan been going?"

"A month or so," Clarissa said. "Ever since she started up."

"Does Madame Swoboda always incorporate numbers in her messages?"

"Numbers? No, not always. Sometimes."

"What do you make of them?"

"Nothing," Clarissa said firmly. "Nothing at all."

"How about Dan?"

"Dan believes in numerology," she said slowly. "He says his lucky number is twelve. If her numbers add up to a divisor or multiple of twelve, he believes that's his day to gamble. I think he loses as fast on those days as the others."

Shayne turned to the Thains. "What do you make of the numbers?"

Percy Thain looked beaten and dispirited; his hostility toward Shayne seemed to be gone. "I don't know. I don't try to understand everything. It's enough for me to hear my son's voice."

"And you?" The redhead shifted his eyes to Mabel.

"They give me a sense of mystic knowledge," she said exaltedly, fastening her eyes on the dark sky as if probing its mysteries. "It is a cabala, the theosophy of the occult. One senses and one knows, but none of these things can be communicated in words."

Shayne waited a moment, tugging his left earlobe, then turned. "I'll keep in touch with you, Mrs. Milford. And don't worry."

Lost in thought, he walked toward the car. Mabel

had, of course, treated the matter of the voodoo doll lightly to keep her sister from being unduly distressed. But Clarissa had said Mabel believed in the seances, therefore she must also believe in the potency of a curse symbolized by a doll.

He patted Lucy's knee when he got in the car and backed it out the drive. Near the shrubbery where he had glimpsed the movement of a few minutes before, he stopped long enough to call softly to Martin on the shag job. "Nice going, Bill. Let me know when Dan Milford—or anybody— comes in."

Out on the road the gray Buick picked up his trail again. He put his arm on Lucy's shoulder, drawing her over so he could feel the warmth of her body beside him. She seemed tense.

"Don't worry, angel. Somebody's going to see me take you home, that's all. And if it's a spy from a morals squad, he can go back and report I didn't eat breakfast at your apartment."

"I'm not worried about that—it's Clarissa."

"She was only crying on my shoulder."

"I know. I feel terribly sorry for her."

"So do I. She's in love with her no-good husband, and from the way it looks now, he's got some of the answers we need."

8

Shayne rose early the next morning, showered, shaved, dressed and ate breakfast and, twenty minutes later, was striding through the downstairs lobby to the door. He stopped suddenly, turned back to the desk, picked up the phone and dialed Sylvester's home.

Mrs. Santos answered, her voice tired and worried. No, Sylvester hadn't come home or called and she didn't know where he was. Shayne pronged the receiver, made for the door again and long-legged it to where he had parked his car the night before.

The gray Buick was parked a few cars behind it. The redhead passed, then whirled impulsively and stared boldly for half a minute at the man behind the wheel. He didn't recognize the face but he would again, undistinctive as it was. The man was about average height with straight black hair thinning a little on top, and lidless eyes, like a snake's. His skin had that peculiarly dry look which comes as the result of a bad case of acne at puberty. He wore a wilted seersucker suit and no hat. Under

Shayne's gaze, he shifted uneasily, lifting one hand to wipe self-consciously at his long upper lip. The hand was thin and bony, with big knuckles and visible veins.

Shayne waved genially, wryly amused at the startled and defensive look the gesture brought, turned and strode to his own car.

Speeding along Biscayne Boulevard, he turned east to the Causeway leading to the Beach. The morning was already hot. Sun beat on the road, making a mirror of it and intensifying the vivid flower colors along its edge. There was no wind. Spanish moss hung stiffly from the trees.

Through the rear-view mirror Shayne kept an eye on the tailing Buick, realizing suddenly that a green car which had pulled out from the curb too when he left his apartment was holding close behind the Buick. Was it possible that, this morning, he had two tails?

He crossed the Causeway and turned south, the two cars still with him, finally pulling in the parking lot at the head of the long slip where Sylvester's boat was moored. Most of the other boats were already out, leaving the *Santa Clara* almost alone.

Near her on the wharf, a tall man was bent over, concentrating on something. As Shayne strode closer he recognized him as Slim, the lazy one from Philadelphia, who had lain on his back all day without doing anything more energetic than tilting a rum highball. He was the do-it-yourself man whose hobby was mechanics, according to Sylvester. This morning he had a different hobby. He was cleaning a fish.

He looked up from the mess of blood and guts as Shayne's shadow fell across him. "Oh, hello, Mike."

"Good morning. Is Sylvester around?"

"No, he's down the coast somewhere. Be gone a day or two, he said."

"What did he do, walk?" Shayne eyed the *Santa Clara*.

"Nope. Got a lift."

"Boat or car?"

There was an instant's hesitation before Slim said, "Car."

"What did he go for?"

"There's a boat he wanted to look at."

"How come?"

"I think he's considering a trade."

"What's the matter with this boat? You boys just put a new engine in her, didn't you?"

"Turned out to be a dog."

"Since yesterday?"

Slim shrugged and went on scraping his fish with the thoroughness of a good Dutch housewife.

"I thought the engine sounded pretty good," Shayne persisted.

"Doesn't develop the speed it ought to. Sylvester said his old one was faster. Sylvester's hell for speed."

"How'd he know? You boys never let him let it out?"

"He did, I guess. When we weren't with him."

"Yesterday he was telling me how good it was."

"That was yesterday. Today he didn't like it. You know how these Portuguese are."

"He's not Portuguese. He's Cuban."

"Same difference."

Shayne was silent. The only sound was the rasping of Slim's heavy knife against the fish scales. Without looking up, Slim said, "This is that grouper you caught yesterday. Hope you don't mind."

"I don't mind."

"Want a piece of him?"

"No."

"Got to thinking—" Slim seemed to feel it necessary to explain—"it's kind of silly to be down here in the world's fishing paradise and never eat any fish. So I came down this morning to get this one. I'll clean it up and have the chef at the hotel cook it for me."

"It's a pretty big fish."

"I'll need it. Some of the boys are coming in to play poker this afternoon. Fish and beer and poker —that ought to be a good combo, huh?"

"Pretty good." Shayne frowned down at the bloody mess on the wharf planks. "You know, they'd clean it for you at the hotel as well as cook it, if you asked them."

"Yeah, but I've got a thing about fish. I got to know they're cleaned good. Never eat 'em unless I clean 'em myself."

"That's a lot of blood from one fish."

"It's a big fish."

"It's still a lot of blood."

Slim shrugged, still not looking up. "I wouldn't know. I heard groupers are running bloody this season."

"Hogwash! A grouper's a grouper, this season or any other."

"Maybe you're right." The knife kept scraping. The scales spattered.

Shayne shot his half-smoked cigarette irritably into the water. A black depression was growing within him. "I think I'll go aboard for a minute."

Slim looked up for almost the first time since the redhead had come. "O.K. Help yourself."

Shayne stepped across and prowled around the cockpit, cabin and deck. It was the same as last night; everything was in place. He leaped from the gunnel back to the dock and then, looking back, he noticed that the coil of rope on the deck forward had no anchor attached to it.

"Where's the anchor?"

Slim had finished cleaning the fish and was lowering a bucket on a rope over the side of the dock to get water to sluice away the blood and fish offal that was already attracting flies. "Anchor ring needed a weld. Somebody picked it up for the fix after we came in last night."

Had the anchor been there when he looked over the boat last night? Shayne couldn't be sure.

As Slim moved in from the dock edge with the bucket of water, Shayne stepped in ahead of him, took off his hat and mopped his forehead. The handkerchief slipped from his hand and landed in the fish blood.

"Too bad," Slim drawled as Shayne bent to pick it up. "Better throw it away. It'll smell like hell of fish."

"It'll wash out." Shayne folded the handkerchief so the blood was inside and returned it to his pocket.

Slim tossed the water forcefully from the bucket onto the bloody planks and turned back to dip up some more.

"Funny how things go," Shayne said. "I ran into Ed last night."

"Yeah? Where?"

"Seance. At Madame Swoboda's."

Slim laughed shortly. "Yeah, his wife goes for that stuff. Sometimes she drags him along."

"You ever go?"

"Once, for kicks. There weren't any."

"You staying at Ed's hotel?"

"Yeah. Blue Grotto."

"What about Vince?"

"He's at the Mirador."

"What's his last name?"

"Becker." Slim gave him a probing look. "Why you so interested all of a sudden?"

"I'm not sure I am, yet." Shayne turned abruptly and started walking back to his car. "See you around."

"O.K." Slim sloshed more water on the wharf.

Before starting the motor Shayne sat staring off

101

over the water, his gray eyes bleak, his face deeply trenched. His feeling of depression had not abated, and now a slow fury grew within him. He thought of Sylvester's neat cabin and of his love for the boat and a lump choked his throat. Still . . . there was nothing rational to go on yet.

He gunned the engine and moved out into the traffic stream headed for the Causeway to Miami. His two tails stayed with him, but they were the least of his worries now. On Biscayne he slammed on the brakes in front of a just-opened bar, parked and went in. He ordered a Hennessy from a pale and disinterested-looking bartender, downed it in one gulp, strode to a phone booth in the rear and scanned the yellow pages of the directory. Only a few blocks away, he found a medical laboratory run by a William Fox.

He heeled out to the car, slid behind the wheel and drove the short distance, stopping in front of a modern white stone and glass building. The tails drove past, averting their eyes with elaborate casualness.

The day was growing hotter. Sweat seeped down inside the redhead's collar, wetting his shirt. It felt icy. He got out of the car and stalked up the walk into the building, went down the hall and through a door marked *William Fox, Laboratories*.

The blond receptionist, startled by his peremptory entrance, looked up from a roll and a paper container of coffee.

"I'd like this blood analyzed." Shayne took the wadded handkerchief from his hip pocket.

"Certainly, sir. But no one's in yet."

"Get someone in! This is urgent!"

Shayne's inner tension and barely-leashed fury, communicated itself to the girl. She stared hypnotized into his stark eyes and her own face whitened. Her fingers tightened on the paper coffee container and she half rose. "I think I just heard Mr. Fox come in. There's a door to the laboratory from the other side."

Before she could protest, Shayne strode past her, thrust open the door behind her desk and entered the laboratory. A stout, graying man, just struggling into a white coat, eyed him with acute disfavor.

"No one's allowed back here. Please wait outside."

Shayne dropped the wadded handkerchief on a bare, white table top. "I've no time for formalities. Analyze this blood." While the man stammered, Shayne added, "I'm investigating a murder."

The technician's eyes bulged. "Are you from the police?"

"What difference does it make? No, I'm not. I'm a private detective."

"I only asked." Fox picked up the handkerchief gingerly and carried it to a laboratory table in front of a window, looking back uneasily. "I don't want to get in any trouble."

Shayne's hands clenched. "What trouble could you get in? If I were the murderer I'd know whether my victim was a man or a fish. And that's all I want you to tell me—whether that's human or fish blood."

Fox turned to the table and began working with tubes, liquids and eyedroppers.

Shayne lit a cigarette and blew smoke in a blue cloud toward the window. After working silently for a few minutes, Fox looked around.

"There's more than a trace of human blood mixed with the fish blood," he said.

"Have you typed it?"

"From first examination, I'd say 'O.' "

"That limits it, anyway. What do I owe you?"

"Ten dollars. Pay the girl, please."

Shayne gave him a bleak nod, turned and went through the door, dropping a ten-dollar bill on the receptionist's desk.

9

From the drugstore downstairs, Shayne called his office.

"I'm dreaming!" Lucy said. "Or are you? Talking in your sleep, I mean?"

"It's the shank of the day, angel."

Sensing the depression beneath his glib words, she asked anxiously, "What is it, Michael?"

"Phone Mrs. Santos and find out Sylvester's doctor. Phone the doctor and see if he has Sylvester's blood type and if he has, if it's Rh. Then phone the information to Peter Painter's office where I'll go from here. Got it?"

"Got it. Michael, is something the matter with Sylvester?"

"I think he's been murdered."

She gasped. "Oh, Michael, I know how you—"

"One thing more," he broke in, keeping his voice matter-of-fact, "has Bill Martin called in a report on Clarissa Milford?"

"Yes. Nothing's happened. She hasn't left the house and no one has gone in."

"Not even her husband?"

"No one, he said."

"Next time Bill phones in, tell him to hang on till I can get somebody to relieve him."

"All right, Michael." She paused. "Whatever it was with Sylvester, is it part of the voodoo doll business?"

"That's something I have to find out. The only connection now is that one of the men I met on Sylvester's boat turned up at Swoboda's seance last night."

"Then there might be—"

"Yes, there might be," he said bleakly and hung up.

Peter Painter had just taken off his coat when Shayne burst into the office. The Detective Chief turned irritably at the early morning intrusion.

Shayne asked humorlessly, "Something bad you ate, Petey? Or is it me?"

Painter sat down behind his desk with bristling officiousness, lifted one hand and traced the thin line of his black mustache with his thumbnail. He did not invite Shayne to be seated. "It's you," he said.

Putting his knuckles on the desk, Shayne leaned toward Painter. "Did you get a phone call this morning that concerns me?"

"I think I've had two. One from your secretary, and one from a William Fox of the William Fox Medical Laboratories. I'm sure Mr. Fox was describing you. 'Paranoiac type,' he said. 'Delusions of grandeur. Probably homicidal.' In fact, he thinks you've already murdered somebody. So do I. Henry Henlein."

"No, it would be William Fox," Shayne said, "except that I didn't have time. What did my secretary say?"

"She wanted me to report to you that Sylvester Santos' blood type is Rh."

Shayne said grimly, "Then I want to report to your office, Painter, what I believe to be the murder of Sylvester Santos. He's been running the *Santa Clara,* a charter boat, for years."

"I know who you mean."

"If you work fast enough before they move it, I think you'll find Sylvester's knife-stabbed body on the harbor bottom, weighted down by his own boat anchor, at the slip where he rents mooring space."

Painter made notes on a pad. "Would it be in order," he asked sarcastically, "for the police department to inquire how citizen Shayne came by this rather precise information?"

"It would be in order," Shayne said evenly, "but I haven't time to tell you. Get going on this, will you?"

"I gather this is of close personal interest to you, shamus." Painter's thin lips stretched in an unctuous smile. "And inasmuch as you're asking me to do something—there was a murder yesterday in which you also were involved . . ."

A muscle twitched in Shayne's cheek. "I can't help you on that one, Petey."

"It's just possible you won't have to, hard as it

will be for you to believe it. Ballistics has reported that he was shot by his own gun."

"That .32 Colt with the walnut handle that was lying beside him?"

Painter nodded.

"That's funny. Henlein was a muscleman. I heard he didn't usually carry a gun."

"That was the rumor. Maybe he bought one and committed suicide."

"Sure. And tied that noose around his own neck. Look, Painter, the one thing I can help you with—Sylvester—you don't seem to want to listen to. If you find him murdered where I told you to look, I can name you three prime suspects."

Painter reached for his pen with simulated weariness, holding it poised and waiting.

"Ed Woodbine, Blue Grotto," Shayne said, "Slim Collins, Blue Grotto, Vince Becker, Mirador. I haven't checked the addresses yet, but I think they're right. These men are putting on a good, honest front."

"What if they are on the up and up?"

"Then we look elsewhere. You might check back where they say they came from. They're vacationists. Ed Woodbine's in the insurance business in Detroit. He's here with his wife. Slim Collins is a contractor with a hobby for working on internal-combustion engines. He's from Philadelphia. Vince Becker owns a motel in Arizona. That's what they told me, anyway. Their names may be phony. Becker looks Sicilian. In fact, none of them fit, but I'll leave the checking to you."

"Your trust is gratifying. However, how do I know all this isn't a red herring you dreamed up to dilute our efforts to probe into the Henlein murder?"

A muscle jumped in Shayne's cheek and his knuckles strained as his big hands gripped the table edge. He fastened his gray eyes on Painter with such bleak savagery that the Detective Chief drew back and lowered his own eyes to the neat pile of papers on his desk. "I don't give a damn about Henlein," Shayne snapped, "but Sylvester was a friend of mine."

"All right," Painter murmured. "I was only asking. Your co-operation with this office isn't always so good, you know."

Shayne swung away. "Phone Lucy at my office when you turn anything up on Sylvester." At the door, he added, "I've got two tails on me this morning. If one of them's yours, you'd better warn him not to get hurt."

"Now look here, Shayne—" Painter half rose, but Shayne was out of sight down the hall.

The redhead stopped at a bar down the street, picked up a double Hennessy and carried it with him to a phone booth. He wanted to see Madame Swoboda again and to talk with Percy and Mabel Thain, but most important of all he wanted to find Clarissa's husband, Dan Milford. Two men had been murdered since yesterday, and Dan Milford was still missing. Perhaps, as his wife feared, *he* had been murdered too, but if he was still alive . . .

He downed the cognac, drew a well-worn address book from his pocket and thumbed through it.

He dialed a number. When the connection was made, he said, "This is Mike Shayne, Bobo. How's the world treating you?"

"It ain't." The voice came sourly. "I'm treating it."

"You got any games going?"

"Naw. Annual clean-up week. The cops closed us."

"Tight?"

"Tight."

"Anybody they haven't got to yet?"

"You might try Harley. His friend on the force works harder for him than mine does."

"Craps or poker?"

"Both, if he's running."

"Thanks. What's his number now?"

"Hang on. . . . Beach 7-9811 . . ."

"Thanks, Bobo." Shayne forked the receiver, unforked it and dialed again. When the line was open he could hear a mumble of male voices and an echoing rattle before a nasal "Hello" came over.

"This is Shayne, Harley. I hear you've got a game running."

"Yeah? You keep your ears flapped out, you hear plenty. Who told you?"

"Bobo."

"So?"

"I'm looking for someone, Harley. Dan Milford. Is he there?"

"How would I know? They're all Joe Doakses to

me, you know what I mean? That's what they write on their phony checks."

"Don't give me that, Harley. You know all of them. You have to, to stay in business. Is Dan Milford there?"

"Look, Shayne, I wouldn't stay in business ten minutes if I handed out names to every cop, wife or private eye who asked me. You know that."

"All I know," Shayne said angrily, "is I'm coming over there and if Dan Milford isn't there because you tipped him that I'm coming, the annual clean-up week will hit you and your police department contact so hard you'll both be out of business—for good!"

"Now wait a minute, shamus. How you going to know if Dan Milford was here or wasn't here if he's gone?"

"I won't. I'll just assume he was and you tipped him. So if he isn't there, go get him. He's in one or another of the floating games, if there's any more left besides yours. I'll be over in fifteen minutes."

Shayne slammed down the receiver, strode out and got in his car and started moving. Harley's place was in an old warehouse on Southwest Fourth Avenue. As the redhead turned south toward the river his thoughts seethed. The gray Buick and the green sedan were still with him. Assume for the moment that Peter Painter had not put a police tail on him. The loan-shark boss, De Luca, had ways of keeping in touch with that part of the Miami world which could affect him. If De Luca knew that Henny Henlein had come to Shayne's office yesterday, De Luca would be worried today. So one of these tails could be his. And if the other had been hired by the three vacationists on Sylvester's boat, it would seem to indicate either that the hoodlum's murder and the murder of Sylvester were unconnected, or that one half of the vengeful group did not know what the other half was doing.

While this speculation was a subterfuge to keep from thinking about Sylvester, agonized thoughts of the little man kept breaking through. He must have been knifed only minutes before Shayne had arrived at the dock. Slim, and any of the others who might have been with him, could have sighted Shayne maneuvering for a parking space in the lot at the head of the slip. They'd have had time to drop Sylvester's body over the side with the anchor weight, then leave while Slim grabbed the grouper from the ice box and began to clean it over the place on the wharf already soaked by Sylvester's blood.

Still, why had they killed Sylvester? Mrs. Santos said Sylvester had been looking for Shayne last night. Had Sylvester known something at that time —something the others couldn't risk having him tell? Or had Shayne's presence on the boat yesterday alarmed them unduly? They might have reasoned that Sylvester had motivated it and that the little man knew something damaging to them which, actually, he didn't. Then too, if they had been suspicious because of Shayne's presence on the boat yesterday, their suspicions of Shayne, and Sylvester, must have zoomed into high when Ed met Shayne at the seance last night, assuming that Ed's presence there was more than coincidental.

If they had felt themselves so imperiled that they had killed Sylvester, wouldn't Shayne now be marked out for early slaughter?

The tailing cars, and the apparently innocuous seance last night, were taking on a more sinister character. Even Henlein's murder, distant as it seemed from the three fishermen, might be interrelated some way. And Clarissa Milford. Where did she fit in this mélange of murder?

Shayne stopped the car, strode across the sidewalk and moved out of sight between two weather-beaten buildings, sagging in the sun. A narrow warehouse door opened in one of them and a short, unshaven man in shirtsleeves, chewing the stump of a cold cigar, stepped out.

"All right, Harley. Where is he?"

The man removed the cigar from his mouth, spat on the sandy ground, put the cigar back and motioned over one shoulder with his thumb. "Inside."

As Shayne moved toward the door, Harley added, "Wait a minute, shamus. I never done this before. I got a favor to ask you."

"What is it?"

"Just don't tell him I was in on this, see? If it got around it could ruin me."

"All right." Shayne turned impatiently. "Your reputation, such as it is, is safe with me."

"To tell the truth, I'll be glad when he's out. He's losin' his shirt."

"I thought that was how you made your living."

"Only when they pay," Harley said sourly. He took the cigar stump out of his mouth and spat again. "This guy gives paper no bank knows."

At a sign from Harley to a suspicious face that had been peering at them through a sliding panel, the door opened and Shayne stepped inside.

"I'm not coming with you," Harley muttered. "You understand?"

"How'll I know Milford?"

"Guy in the blue shirt. At the poker table."

Shayne lounged across the room casually, stopping at the craps table, and stood listening to the jumbled groans, chuckles and exhortations as the dice rolled. It was a game of high stakes, as most of these continuous games were, and the tension of it showed in the lined faces, sweating brows and tired eyes of the gamblers. Only the stickmen seemed unperturbed.

After a moment, the redhead wandered on to the poker table, stopping behind the chair of the man in the blue shirt.

"Move, fella, will you?" Milford said petulantly. "You'll jinx me."

"You're already jinxed." Shayne eyed the small stack of white chips. "Get yourself dealt out. I want to talk to you."

Milford turned to look squarely at Shayne. He was heavily built, with a sad, ruddy face and pale blue eyes, a big sheep-dog of a man, neither the prototype of a murderer, nor the great lover Clarissa had led Shayne to expect.

He shook his head almost helplessly and sighed. "Deal me out, Gus."

Leaving the few white chips lying on the table, he pushed back his chair and stood up clumsily. He was over six feet tall, his eyes on a level with Shayne's. Like a man sleep-walking, he moved to a worn mohair davenport flanked by standing ash trays and spittoons, sat down without speaking and buried his face in his hands, the picture of a man in utter dejection and total defeat.

After a moment he raised his head slightly and looked through his fingers at Shayne. "What are you waiting for? Let's get going."

"Where?"

"Out to the alley. Or to the car. Or wherever you plan on doing it."

Shayne said, "I have no plans. Who do you think I am?"

"You're from D. L. I know."

"No, I'm not. I came on my own to help you, or maybe to get you to help me. Someone has threatened to kill your wife."

Milford stared. It took an instant for the words to penetrate. Shayne watched in cynical dispassion as fear and anger in slow succession, and lastly something that might have been remorse, filled the pale and red-veined eyes. Finally big tears squeezed from between his lids and rolled untended down his face.

"Oh, God!" Milford said.

10

Shayne sat down on the davenport as Milford rose and towered above him, clenching his big fists and beating them futilely against his thighs. "The bastards! I'll kill them first!"

"One has been killed," Shayne said evenly. "Henny Henlein."

"Henny's not enough. Henny's nothing. It's the big ones—" Milford stopped suddenly, fighting for control.

"Did you kill Henlein?"

"No." Sanity seemed to be returning. Milford blinked fiercely at the redhead, asking, "Who are you?"

"Mike Shayne. How long have you been sitting in this game?"

"Since before Henlein was murdered, if that's what's on your mind."

"How do you know when Henlein was murdered?"

"I heard it on the radio here."

"Can you prove it?"

Milford fastened raging eyes on Shayne, as

though he were the source of all his misery. "I wish to God I *had* killed Henny. I wish I had, by God! He's the one who threatened Clarissa—"

"Sending a voodoo doll doesn't seem quite in line with Henny's method of operation, or D. L.'s either."

Milford stared in what seemed like genuine perplexity.

"Somebody left your wife one, stabbed through the heart with a black-headed pin."

"God! She didn't tell me."

"Somebody sent Henlein a couple too—one stabbed and one strangled—and then followed it up by murdering him and leaving him with a hang-rope around his neck."

Milford looked dazed. He rubbed his big hands over his face, pushing at his eyes, then said slowly, "De Luca told me something would happen to Clarissa if I didn't get up the money by twelve tonight. I thought he was trying to scare me—"

"How much do you owe him?"

"Around four thousand."

"Have you got it?"

"No, and I never will now. My luck's gone bad."

"You thought you'd get it here? In Harley's rigged game?"

"I didn't know any other way."

"You sure?"

"I'm sure."

Shayne was watching Milford through lidded eyes. "Your wife's life insurance would more than cover it."

The big man eyed Shayne with such flaming rage that for a moment the redhead thought he was going to have a fight on his hands. "Isn't your indignation a little forced," he prodded. "I understand you wanted a divorce—"

Milford clenched his fists so tightly the veins bulged, then suddenly his body went limp. He dropped to the davenport and sagged forward, burying his face in his hands again and speaking in a muffled voice through his fingers. "I did it to protect her. I thought if D. L. got the idea she didn't mean anything to me, she would be safe. I thought he wouldn't try to get at me through her. I guess I was wrong."

"What about Madame Swoboda?"

"What about her?"

"Your wife thinks you're in love with her."

"I let her think that." Milford uncovered his face, looking at Shayne in undiluted misery. "I didn't know what else to do. I had to make my wife break away from me for her own safety. You can see that, can't you?"

"I suppose so."

"But it isn't true that I didn't love her," Milford cried. "I do love her. I always will. She's the only one I'll ever love."

Despite the fact that Shayne had not expected to like Dan Milford, he was finding that he did. At least, he pitied him and pity was close to liking. Milford showed an unexpected honesty and, out of keeping with his size, a humbleness. It was easier now to understand Clarissa's stubborn love, even though Milford had tried to make her think that he loved another woman.

However, emotions should not influence judgments. No matter how convincingly he might talk about his love for Clarissa, the hard fact remained that her insurance money would get him out of a bad spot and, apparently, it was the only thing that would.

To determine just how bad the spot was, Shayne asked, "What happens now that you can't pay off D. L.?"

Milford said, almost inaudibly, "He'll kill me, I think. He might have been contented with working me over for a long hospital stay, but now with his muscleman murdered—he'll blame me for that—"

"Why not go to the police? Get protection?"

Milford faced the detective squarely, his jaws drooping, his mouth twisted. "What's the use? They can't watch over me all my life. Myself, I don't deserve it anyway. But I'll go to them for Clarissa, now that I know."

"Don't worry about Clarissa. She hired me to find out who sent her the voodoo doll, and I'm having her guarded."

"Thanks, Mr. Shayne."

"Do you think it's possible," the redhead asked, drawing out a cigarette and lighting it, "that your brother-in-law believes it was Clarissa who ran over his son?"

"Why would he think it was Clarissa?"

"It was Clarissa's car. The hit-and-run driver hasn't been identified. Why couldn't it have been Clarissa?"

"I'll tell you why it couldn't. Clarissa had the set of keys she always uses in her purse. She always kept an extra set hidden in the car—ever since she got locked out of her car one time."

"Where in the car?"

"I don't know."

"So when the car was found abandoned, it was the extra set of keys that was in it?"

Milford nodded.

"Did anyone tell that to the police who investigated the accident?"

"Maybe. I don't know. Anyway, it was obvious that the car thief found the hidden keys."

Shayne said, "Let's come back to Percy Thain. Wouldn't you say sending a voodoo doll seems more characteristic of him than of D. L. or his muscle-men?"

"Yes. Only why would he stab Henlein? I don't think he ever heard of Henny Henlein."

"Who said Henlein was stabbed?" Shayne asked quietly.

"Didn't you?"

"I said one of the voodoo dolls he received was stabbed, and one was strangled. Henny Henlein was shot—with his own gun."

Milford's face grayed. "With his own gun," he repeated dully. "Was it a .32 Colt with the corrugations on the walnut handle cut off on the lower side?"

Shayne's gray eyes held on Milford with quickened interest. "I could find that out. At the police station they told me the gun had been positively identified as Henlein's."

"Mr. Shayne, I'm going to level with you. You say you've put protection on my wife and I'm grateful. And anyway, I've gambled and lost, and lied to Clarissa about Madame Swoboda, and I'm in debt to a loan-shark who is undoubtedly going to kill me, so what have I got to lose by a little involvement in Henny's murder?"

"I thought you said you weren't involved."

"I didn't kill him. But last week I took his gun away, when he came threatening me with it for De Luca."

"What did you do with the gun?"

"Took it home. Put it in a dresser drawer. I haven't looked for it since. I thought it was still there."

Shayne dropped his cigarette butt into a spittoon. "I suppose you know what you're saying. The person most likely to find it there would be your wife."

"That's not what I'm saying," Milford denied loudly. "You must be crazy if you think Clarissa would, or could, kill Henlein."

"She had good reason. She knew you were in up to your ears with D. L. So maybe Henny threatened her. Maybe he ordered her to meet him and she took the gun along, just in case—"

"If you think that—" Milford rose suddenly, glaring down at Shayne. "I don't want you to have any

121

more to do with her. We'll hire someone else—"

"Take it easy. I don't think Clarissa killed Henlein. He got two dolls and she got one. I think the same person sent them all."

"Then why'd you say that?"

"I thought *you* were trying to make me think she killed him."

"God, no," Milford said huskily. "I love my wife."

"You've a poor way of showing it. She's worried sick about you. Go home to her."

"How can I? I'm broke. She thinks I don't love her—"

"Even a married man can kiss his wife," Shayne said, his gray eyes bright. "One kiss will take care of everything. All she wants is you."

He rose and walked away, past the poker table and the dice table, and some of Shayne's heartsick anger about Sylvester spilled over to touch Dan Milford. Somehow, he still couldn't help liking the man.

11

Shayne got into the car, swung around in the middle of the block and turned north. An unpeopled silence had been about him when he left the river, but as he approached the center of town the tempo of city noises increased and when he parked, the hum of life was around him.

It was well known in certain circles that the loan-shark racketeer, De Luca, headquartered at a place called Joe's Bar, near Southeast First and Flagler.

Inside Joe's he ordered a Hennessy, turned sideways and leaned one elbow on the bar while he surveyed the long smoky room. Despite the fact that D. L. was known to be tops in mobster money, Joe's Bar looked no more plush than a thousand others.

The room was half full, three men at the bar beside himself and five or six more in booths at the side. In the rear, next to the cigarette machine, a man slouched against a door, seemingly unconcerned, but obviously on guard. Downing the cognac, Shayne left a bill on the bar and walked over to him.

"Where do I see D. L.?" The redhead put coins into the cigarette machine and pulled a handle. With a tinkle and a thud the cigarettes dropped down.

The man looked at Shayne expressionlessly. The skin on his face was ridged and flaking, much like that of the man who had been tailing Shayne in the gray Buick. Acne was either an occupational disease of gangsters, or the result of childhood malnutrition.

"He ain't in." The words were insolently mouthed, the stream of smoke in Shayne's face a calculated challenge.

"Then why are you playing bulldog?" With a violent yank Shayne grabbed the man's coat collar in his big hands and pulled him close, holding him dangling with his heels off the floor as though he were a dog on a short leash. Then suddenly he released him with a shove that sent him thudding against the door.

The man swore viciously and, bracing his shoulders against the door, aimed a disabling kick at Shayne's groin. The redhead stepped aside, throwing his own heel sideways and connecting with the guard's knee. The man let out a yelp of pain. Shayne broke the sound midway with a short-armed jab that slammed his head against the door again.

One of the bartenders slid under the bar and moved in fast. The redhead stepped inside a murderously aimed leather sap and put two jabs to the flabby stomach. The bartender bent double, gasping. On the instant, the guard at the door slashed out with a switchblade knife. It cut only air before Shayne had the knife wrist in the vise of his big fist. With something tangible to vent his anger on, he crashed his other fist into the man's jaw, watching him hang against the wall a moment before his body sagged and he slid to the floor in a crumpled heap, his eyes blank and empty.

Another man was moving from the bar when the door to D. L.'s office opened, and a quiet voice said, "Let him come in, Max."

Shayne stepped over the unconscious guard and the crime chief closed the door behind him.

If the front of Joe's Bar was not plush, the same could not be said of D. L.'s private office. Here the walls were covered with red velvet with a silken sheen. The furniture, even to the massive French desk, was a shiny gold. A four-foot crystal chandelier suspended from the ceiling reflected the colors in its ever-moving prisms with a dazzling effect.

Amid all this splendor the man in the room wore a rumpled white shirt that had an elongated coffee stain down the front. His collar was half open, his sleeves rolled up, his tie awry. He padded across the oriental rug to his desk where he squatted like a frog, smiling ironically and flashing gold fillings which matched the furniture.

The man from whom De Luca had inherited this loan-shark empire was dead and moldering—if not by De Luca's hand, then by his direction. And lucrative as was the loan-shark racket in Miami, it was generally thought to be only a sideline with De

Luca, and that his real profit came from narcotics smuggling. He master-minded the details of bringing it into the country for the Syndicate and seeing it safely on its way to cutting and distributing centers in the North. It was rumored that he had known Lucky Luciano before Luciano was deported to Italy, and had since visited with the dope and vice czar there. However, as yet no crimes of consequence had been hung on De Luca by local or federal lawmen, for he was cunning and capable as well as ruthless.

"I was expecting you, Mr. Shayne," De Luca said in a soft voice, "though I was hardly prepared for such a violent entry. I deplore violence."

Shayne said dryly, "Then you ought to teach your goon some manners." He rubbed his knuckles and followed De Luca to the desk.

"My goon, as you inelegantly put it, is an ignoramus. Good muscles, though. Still, yours must be better. I admire both the mental and the physical."

"Red velvet and gold don't seem conducive to good muscles."

"They aren't. I haven't good muscles myself. But I admire beauty too."

"Such as Madame Swoboda's?"

Shayne sat down on a red-velvet-upholstered chair beside the desk, eying the rumpled shirt with the coffee-colored stain. De Luca's head reflected the red and gold lights almost as sharply as the chandelier prisms. His face was soft and round, his dark eyes puffy, his nose and mouth fat. Protruding

126

and unsymmetrical ears broke the circular effect, emphasizing the only slight difference between the width of his face and his bull-like neck.

"Madame Swoboda? I don't think I know her." D. L. sounded contrite. "Ought I to?"

"She's beautiful."

"And she runs a whorehouse in Miami?" He looked honestly incredulous.

"She's not that kind of madam." Shayne played it straight. "Madame Swoboda's a mystic. She holds seances and communicates with the spirit world."

"I'm sure I never heard of her."

"One of your musclemen must have known her. Henny Henlein."

"Ah, yes. Poor Henny." D. L. opened an ebony box on the desk and pushed it toward Shayne. The redhead shook his head and took a cigarette from his pocket. D. L. reached into the box himself, removed a cigar from its little wooden coffin, bit off the end and spat it carefully over the shoulder away from Shayne. He lit it from an ornamental desk lighter and leaned back in the ornate chair. "That was very unfortunate. You didn't do it, did you?"

"No."

"I heard the police thought you did. Henny had your address in his pocket."

"Henny tried to hire me. *You* didn't have him killed, did you?"

"Don't you know yet?" D. L. blew a billow of smoke at the ceiling. "I thought you'd have it all unraveled by now. One just can't believe everything one hears about the miracles private detectives perform."

"You didn't answer my question."

"My dear Mr. Shayne, Henny was one of my most valued—henchmen, I believe you'd call him. Not mentally, of course. Mentally, he was an imbecile. But he had beautiful muscles."

"Who killed him?"

"I haven't the slightest idea. There's always an occupational incentive, of course, for a man like Henny to branch out on his own. Being stupid, he would have muffed it. Whoever he was doing it to probably killed him."

"And who was that?"

"I've told you I don't know. It certainly wasn't anyone around here. We all loved him. He had a little-boy quality."

"Maybe that's why someone sent him two voodoo dolls to play with."

"Voodoo dolls?" D. L. looked honestly bemused. "I didn't know about that."

"Your organization's slipping. Why did you think he came to me?"

"To get protection from Dan Milford, of course."

Shayne laughed shortly. "What about his beautiful muscles? Couldn't he protect himself?"

"Henny didn't have confidence," D. L. said regretfully. "If he was on the aggressive end he was all right, but let someone give him a nasty look or threaten him and he went to pieces. That was part of his little boyishness. He was a good man otherwise, but I had to let him carry a gun once in a while to bolster his morale. When Milford took his gun away, it did something to him. Milford was a lot bigger, of course. It was nothing to be ashamed of."

"Speaking of Milford, how much does he owe you?"

"Without checking my books, I'd say over forty-six hundred."

"He thinks it's around four thousand."

"He's forgotten some of the interest," D. L. said in a velvet voice. "They always do. Most people are very poor at figures."

"Just very poor, I'd say—after they pay your interest. I don't think you'll get anything from Milford. He's stony."

"His deadline's midnight tonight." D. L. shrugged elaborately. "People always keep their commitments to me."

"Or else?"

The black eyes in their fleshpots hardened fleetingly, but the voice stayed as unctuously soft as ever. "I'm not a movie villain, Mr. Shayne. I'm a respectable man in a legitimate and socially useful business. The ancient practice of money lending." Once more he gave that brilliant, gold-toothed smile. "And now, will you join me in a drink?"

"A short brandy."

D. L. rose—he was barely five feet tall—and opened a paneled door which hid an ornate bar.

"Do you know Sylvester Santos?" Shayne asked casually. "He runs a charter boat on the Beach."

"No, afraid not. I never fish. I don't believe in

killing for sport." D. L. poured three fingers of cognac into a small glass for each of them.

"Only for business?" Shayne took the glass D. L. extended.

De Luca's eyes glinted dangerously, but his voice held only soft reproach. "Mr. Shayne, you misjudge me."

"Sorry. Then I don't suppose you know the three men who have been chartering Sylvester's boat." Shayne sniffed the brandy. It was old and mellow.

"Are they worth knowing?"

"They killed Sylvester."

The black eyes widened, the thick lips pursed in disapproval and, for the first time, the velvet voice was harsh. "Murderers! They should be apprehended and jailed."

Shayne's voice was hard, his eyes bleak. "They will be."

D. L. regarded him thoughtfully. "This murder means something to you personally?"

"Sylvester was my friend."

D. L. nodded gravely. "Let me ask you a question. He was not, as they crassly say, implicated in the rackets?"

"He was not."

"Then why would they kill a charter-boat captain?"

"When I find that out for sure, I'll have the rest of it. Let's get back to Dan Milford. Henny tried to hire me for the same reason Dan Milford's wife did. She received a voodoo doll like Henny's. And I've been told that you, through Henny, threatened her with violence if her husband didn't pay up."

"That isn't true," D. L. said curtly. With a quick change of expression he smiled across at Shayne, showing a flash of gold teeth. He raised his glass. "To your success," he said and drained the cognac.

"My success might mean your failure." Shayne emptied his glass and set it on a corner of D. L.'s desk.

"Really, Mr. Shayne, I don't understand your attitude," D. L. said petulantly. "I've demonstrated to you that I am conducting a necessary service. When people are desperate for money, deserted by friends, coldly ignored by banks, I help them. My interest rates may be a trifle higher than the law allows, but everyone evades the law in some minor way."

"If you're so socially acceptable, why keep this stable of men with beautiful muscles?"

"They protect me. The best way to make an enemy is to do a favor for a friend, you know. People who can't meet their obligations get vicious sometimes. And as I've told you, I have no muscles myself."

Shayne rose and stood looking down at the squat gangster. "The ancient practice of money lending has prospered lately?"

D. L. nodded agreeably. "Business has prospered gratifyingly the last few months."

"You've had more time to devote to the loan business then," Shayne asked with deceptive quietness, "since the Feds came in and dried up Miami as an entry port for smuggled dope?"

De Luca's eyes glowed with something close to menace. "If you read the newspapers, Mr. Shayne, you are aware that investigation failed to connect my offices in any way with dope running."

"I'm aware that you beat the rap," Shayne said brusquely and moved across the oriental rug to the door. "A final question. Where did Dan Milford expect to get the money by twelve o'clock tonight?"

D. L. got up and clumped after him. "It is not my practice to pry into the personal affairs of my clients. I do not ask how or where they get money —only that they do get it."

"And by the hour agreed upon?"

"By the hour agreed upon, yes."

"Before I go, De Luca," Shayne's voice was hard, "I want to say that if any violence comes to either Dan Milford or his wife you'll answer personally for it."

D. L. raised his eyebrows. "You're threatening me, Mr. Shayne."

"I'm threatening you! By the way, instruct your tail not to make himself so obvious. I might be tempted to work him over with a thoroughness even you will admire."

Surprisingly, D. L. grinned. "Now that we've had our clarifying talk, I may pull him off entirely. Incidentally, he reports you have another tail."

Shayne said dryly, "They're practically scraping fenders."

"The police, I presume?"

"Your guess is as good as mine." Shayne opened the door. Max had revived enough to be standing guard again, but he showed the signs of Shayne's rough handling.

Still in the velvet voice, but with a knife edge beneath it, D. L. said, "You'd better step around to McGloflin's Gym, Max. Build yourself up. Mr. Shayne says you're getting flabby."

Shayne grinned, walked past the glowering guard and out to his car. Once in it he lit a cigarette and staring bleakly ahead, wondering if the visit had paid off. Shayne lifted one big hand and gently massaged his left earlobe between thumb and forefinger. Then abruptly he came to life and tromped on the starter.

Only one tail, the gray Buick, moved out behind him as he swung away from the curb. De Luca had lost no time in getting word to his man to give up the chase.

The lone tail stayed discreetly far behind, almost as if he missed his companion.

Shayne stopped in front of a drugstore, strode in and dialed his office number, making the call he had been dreading to make all morning.

Lucy said, "Michael Shayne's office," and he could tell from her voice what the answer was, but he had to ask anyway.

"I've been expecting a call from Beach police headquarters," he said quietly. "Did Peter Painter call—about Sylvester?"

12

"Yes, Michael," Lucy said softly.

Shayne drove the next question hard. "Was it the way I thought?"

"Yes. They grappled where you told them to, at the end of the wharf by the boat. The body was— Sylvester's body was knifed and weighted down by the *Santa Clara's* anchor, as you guessed."

"Did Painter report on the three suspects I described to him?"

"Yes. They've all been questioned."

"Did he hold them?"

"No."

"Why didn't he?"

" 'No proof,' he said. 'No motive.' "

"What does he want? Has he got to see it happen?"

"Wait, darling," Lucy said gently, "there's more."

"Let's have it."

"It's interesting, and disturbing. When Painter checked on the three men he discovered they had all been under observation by his office. They're criminals of record, and they've all served time, but they checked in at the police station like good boys when they arrived, the way the rules say. They're here on a vacation, that's all—"

"According to Painter!" Shayne put in angrily.

"I know. But this is what I thought so curious. They arrived in Miami at about the same time and from different parts of the U. S. Yet they've been inseparable since."

"What criminal records do they have?"

"They're all 'syndicate' men, but there's nothing to show that they ever worked with each other before, or even knew each other."

"What are they working at here?"

"Apparently nothing. Painter had them watched for a few days, thinking they had a job lined up. But they just go fishing, that's all. Painter thinks they're setting up a time-and-place alibi here for something that's happened or is going to happen somewhere else."

"Sylvester wasn't somewhere else," Shayne said bleakly. "Neither was Henny Henlein. And Clarissa and Dan Milford aren't either."

"You think it's all connected?"

"I'm not sure. It seems to be."

"He was such a good little man," Lucy said, as if Shayne had spoken only of Sylvester. Indignation at the violence that had been done to his friend had never been buried far beneath Shayne's words.

"I've got to go now, angel. I'll keep in touch."

The redhead hung up, fished for another coin and dialed Peter Painter.

"I've just talked to Lucy," he said when the

135

Detective Chief answered. "She told me what you reported about Sylvester and our three prime suspects."

"What else do you want to know?"

"Have any of the three contacted De Luca since they've been here, or hobnobbed with any of his hoods?"

"No, not to our knowledge—and I think we'd know. They've kept their noses clean in this town. Fishing. Just fishing."

"Has your office dossiers on them? What about their back-home specialties?"

"Just a minute. I've got it here." Shayne heard the rustle of papers. "The one signed on the hotel register as Collins from Philadelphia—he's from Philly all right—is known there as Tony 'Slim' Rizzo. Stolen-car racket. Served three stretches when he was younger, but now has connections. Used to be good at working on engines. He'd do the work himself, remodel and resell—"

"That's enough. What about Vince Becker?"

"In Arizona he's Joe Arminetti. He's got a boat-yard on Cougar Butte Lake. A front for a race-wire room. Also in slot machines and numbers."

"Can he handle a boat?"

"That's his sport. Yes."

"Ed Woodbine?"

"Slug Murphy in Detroit. Ed 'Slug' Murphy. Labor slugger and union organizer. You know what kind of unions."

"Any of them ever known to do any fishing before?"

"Not as far's I know."

"What about Ed's wife?"

"She is. He's married to her, that is. Edna Appinger, an old-time con woman."

"Lucy says you didn't hold any of them."

"What am I going to hold them on? There's no police pick-up on them from anywhere. And, like I say, they've kept their noses clean here."

"Except for that little item of murder."

"The fact that they had been chartering Sylvester's boat"—Painter's voice rose—"was enough to bring them in for questioning. It certainly isn't enough to book them for murder. We've gone over their persons, their cabanas and the boat. They're all clean."

"The wharf wasn't clean," Shayne said grimly, "where Slim Collins gutted the fish."

"He explained about that. The blood was on the wharf when he came down to get the fish. He didn't want to make any more mess than necessary, so he cleaned his fish where the other blood was—fish blood, he assumed."

"And you bought that?" Shayne asked icily.

"In the absence of motive or any other incriminating evidence, yes," Painter flared. "We bought it."

"How much blood do you think a fish makes?"

"I didn't see it."

"I did."

"Then round up some other evidence to go with it, and maybe you can make something out of it."

"I've been under the vague impression that was police work."

"We've made our investigation. We're satisfied."

"Did any of your men," Shayne asked acidly, "notice that a new engine had been put in Sylvester's boat? And, if they did, did they ask themselves why? Or where a poor Cuban got the money? Or if he didn't get the engine himself, who got it for him? And dirtied it up to look like an old one?"

"Look, Shayne, if you knew all these things why didn't you tell me this morning?"

"I had trouble getting you to listen to what I did tell you. Your three hoodlum vacationers put that engine in Sylvester's boat. Sylvester thought it was because they liked him."

"Maybe it was. You've been shamusing for so long you've forgotten that the milk of human kindness does run in the veins of some people." Painter laughed dryly.

"Is that why you have a tail on me? To protect me—out of kindness?"

"I haven't, you egotist. You asked me that before. What do I care where you go? Just keep out of the way of police department investigations."

"I'll do better than that. You can sit back in your swivel chair and wait while I do your job for you."

Shayne hung up, his gaunt face bleak and deeply trenched.

Three men, engaged in different and unconnected criminal operations, had come to Miami at the same time from three different parts of the country, had chummed up and pretended to go fishing

138

and had murdered Sylvester. One of the men, conveniently, was an expert mechanic and he had put a new engine in Sylvester's boat; another was adept at handling a boat. Shayne had seen him bring the *Santa Clara* to berth with nearly as sure a touch as Sylvester's. The third, genial Ed Woodbine, seemed to have served no function as yet.

Things seemed to funnel from diverse directions to one point—Madame Swoboda. Ed Woodbine had attended a seance; Clarissa Milford and Henlein had both received voodoo dolls.

Shayne stepped on the starter abruptly and turned south toward the Miami River and the last decaying house on a moldering street.

The gray Buick held a wary distance behind him, passing as he parked in front of Swoboda's. It didn't come back. Shayne stepped out of his car to the deserted street and strode toward the rotting yellow house.

By daylight it looked even more precariously placed than it had the night before. The stilts which supported it on the river side were sagging and covered with slimy moss. One piling had split and, in a makeshift effort to keep the house still standing, someone had bound it with rope. The rope stretched and creaked as the water lapped at the piling.

This was the only occupied house on the block. The others, in only slightly more disrepair, stood empty, condemned, their windows gaping and broken, eyeless, in a sort of mute envy of the flicker of life which still existed around them.

The redhead strode back, took a .38 from the glove compartment of the car and dropped it into his side pocket, then again crossed the sinking flagstones with an animal litheness at variance with his bony height. Though the sign beside the heavy pine door still read *Walk in,* he pushed the button.

Nothing happened. He flattened his thumb on the bell button and held it there. Finally the door was opened by Madame Swoboda. Her ebony hair lay smooth and shining in a long pageboy bob and her skin was ivory white against it. The gray, black-lashed eyes looked even more beautiful in the light of day than they had last night.

When she recognized Shayne, her face stiffened. "What do *you* want?"

She made a quick move to close the door but Shayne blocked it and stepped inside.

"This is—illegal!" She was seething. "I'll have you thrown out!"

Shayne moved his eyes over her body. She was wearing a trim tweed skirt and a blouse which, though severely tailored, accented the sexy swell of her breasts, her narrow waist and the exciting curve of hips and thighs. Except for that intense female-ness, however, she looked like any girl on her way to the supermarket, or perhaps to a golf game. Her appearance today was so far removed from what it had been at the seance table that it was hard to believe she had been the "mystic channel" through which messages had flowed from the "other world."

Behind her, several pieces of expensive-looking luggage were stacked against the wall.

"Going some place?"

She bit her lush lips. "It's no concern of yours!"

"I'd hate to lose you just as we've become acquainted." The redhead walked past her into the waiting room and sat down on one of the hard benches. His big hand patted the seat beside him invitingly.

After a moment's hesitation, she came over and sat down. "Now," she said coldly, "why did you force your way in?"

"It's the brute in me. Do you admire brute strength, like D. L.?"

"Is that cryptic remark supposed to mean something to me?"

"You know D. L., of course."

"No, I don't." She widened her round gray eyes and accepted the cigarette he offered, keeping them fastened provocatively on his face and leaning closer than necessary while he lit it. "What do you really want with me?"

"Besides the obvious, I'd like to know who set you up here and why." He was aware of the warmth of her thigh.

"You asked me that before," she said shortly, "and I told you I set myself up. And the reason is apparent."

"Not to me. Let's come at it from another direction, then. What was the meaning of those numbers on Jimsey's tape at last night's seance?"

"Tape?" Her face was blandly innocent. "Do you mean the message from 'outside'?"

"Let's drop the act. It was a message all right—

141

from inside! It was information in some sort of cabala. What was the message? Who was it for?"

"In numerology there is a mystic meaning to all numbers." Her voice was rarefied. "What those particular numbers meant, I do not know. I am only the—magnet which attracts the spirits. The person for whom the message was meant would know."

"Since the voice was supposed to be from the spirit of the boy, Jimsey, the message was meant for his parents, the Thains. Did they understand?"

"Of course."

"I don't think they did. I think those numbers were incorporated in Thain's message for someone else. I want you to tell me who it was."

"I wouldn't know. Different people attend my seances every night. Except for a few regulars I don't know any of them."

"Where did you get the numbers?"

"They came to me in my trance."

"Now look." Shayne's voice hardened. *"You* didn't say anything in what you call your 'trance.' Those messages were prepared beforehand on tape, and both you and I know it."

"Well," she took a deep drag on her cigarette, "what of it? I give them a good show. They get their money's worth in entertainment."

"They get more than their money's worth. You could charge more. Why don't you?"

"Because I'm not greedy," she snapped.

He held her with his eyes. "I think you are—for everything." He saw the rise and fall of her breasts beneath the silken blouse. Slowly, she moved one hand and rested it on his knee. The pressure was light, but he could feel the warmth of her tapering fingers.

For a moment Shayne wondered—would Dan Milford, or any man, resist her female appeal? Had he been too ready to believe Dan Milford's assertion that he loved only his wife?

With a curious detachment, he saw that the roots of her hair were light and her skin too creamy for the ebony hair. Evidently Madame Swoboda had reversed the usual process and dyed her naturally blond hair, black.

Experimentally, he pulled her over, pressing a hard kiss on her lips. They pulsed. Her breathing quickened and Shayne felt her hands creep across his chest, her nails digging through his shirt.

It might have been the creak of a board in the moldering house, or because she opened her eyes to look beyond his shoulder into the opened doorway of the darkened seance room. Or perhaps it was a sixth sense of animal preservation that the redhead had acquired during a lifetime of professional sleuthing.

In a single burst of action he was out of her arms, crouched with one knee on the floor and his gun in his hand.

The two guns spoke at nearly the same instant, their combined echoes breaking flatly in the barren space.

The bullet aimed at Shayne went over his head and splintered the plastered wall. Shayne's shot was precise. The man who had come from the dimness of the seance room heeled back as the bullet drove into his rib casing. The gun dropped from his hand, and both hands pressed hard over the spreading blood.

13

The figure stumped toward them into the light of the waiting room. Blood seeped from between the man's fingers where he held his hands tight-pressed, his face was white and contorted. It was the acned face of the man who had been tailing Shayne since last night in the gray Buick.

"Who hired you?" Shayne drove at him.

"Get me to a hospital!" The words rasped hoarsely.

"Who hired you?"

"I'm bleeding to death, I tell you!"

"You'll live—if we get you to a hospital in time. Who hired you?"

"Some guy . . . didn't tell me his name."

"Do you know D. L.?"

"Who doesn't?"

"Are you working for him?"

"Hell, no. I'm an independent. So's the man that hired me."

"How do you know?"

"He was afraid of D. L. I had instructions to stay clear of D. L. or any of his boys."

"Describe the man who hired you."

"I can't. Medium size is all I know. He was wearing dark glasses."

"Are you working with the other tail?"

"No. Don't know him. For God's sake, quit blabbing and get me to a doc."

"Were you hired to tail me or kill me?"

"At first, just to tail—"

"When did they change the instructions? Before you tailed me to the boat this morning, or afterward?"

"Afterward. I was to take you out if you done certain things."

"What things?"

"Comin' here."

"How do you contact the man who hired you?"

"I don't any more. Dunno where to find him. He's paying me off by mail—he says."

"When?"

"Tomorrow, he says." The man moaned again and sank to one of the benches. "Can't we go now?"

Shayne nodded bleakly. "As soon as I wind things up with the Madame." He turned to the girl whose face was nearly as pale now as the wounded man's. "Who wants to keep me away from you so badly he'd kill me?"

"I don't know! I don't know anything about this."

"Put a call through to police headquarters." He jerked his head toward the phone on the desk.

"Shayne!" She was pleading, desperately. "It's the God's truth! I don't know—"

146

"When you get the police, tell them we've got a gun-shot man here."

"Oh—" She moved toward the phone, looking relieved. "Thank you."

"But whether the cops take you with them, depends on how fast you talk before they get here."

She made the call sullenly and walked back.

Shayne eyed the luggage stacked in the hall. "Why were you running away?"

"It's you and your goddam investigating!" She blazed at him, white-faced and defensive. "It was bound to bring the police in."

"You're clean with the police. I've checked. And you explained last night how legitimately you're operating here."

"Who wants to be mixed up with the police anyway?"

"If you don't, keep talking! Because since I left you last night another man's been murdered—this time a friend of mine."

"Oh, I'm sorry, Shayne." Her voice took on its deep timbre. "I suppose he had one of my voodoo dolls in his pocket," she added in a hurt tone.

"No, but I think he was murdered by one of your regulars—Ed Woodbine, better known in Detroit as Slug Murphy."

"You must believe me! I don't know anything about it." She sat down slowly and looked directly at him without provocativeness, but with a kind of suspended fear. When she spoke it was as if she were talking to herself.

"He told me there was no risk when he set me up."

"Who told you?"

She shrugged fatalistically. "I was doing a mind-reading act in a second-rate club in Vegas, and a gentleman who asked me to have a drink with him one night suggested this. His name was John Smith."

Shayne snorted. "Captain John Smith, no doubt."

"I knew it was a phony, but what difference did it make? He gave me cash—more than I'd ever seen —and told me to come here and rent a house and start the seances. All I'd ever have to do, he said, aside from my regular business, was to work certain numbers into my spirit messages. He didn't tell me what they were for, and I didn't ask."

"Where do you get the numbers?"

"If he's got me into trouble," she said through clenched teeth, "I'll find him and squeeze him dry!" She paused, continuing after a moment with weary resignation. "They come by mail written on a plain sheet of paper in a plain envelope. The postmark is New York City."

"How are they written?"

"Typed, and in the order to be given."

"Has John Smith," Shayne emphasized the name disdainfully, "given you more money since?"

"Yes. Cash sometimes, in the envelopes."

"What do you think the numbers are for?"

She shrugged again. "I suspect I'm a go-between for some sort of Syndicate deal. Policy numbers maybe, or race-track betting. It could be anything,

I guess. I don't know and I don't want to know."

"Have you had any dealings with De Luca?"

"No."

"Did John Smith put any restrictions on you?"

"No-o— Except to keep the seances light entertainment and not to gouge the customers."

"Do you know why that was?"

"He didn't want to attract the attention of the police to his other operation, I guess—whatever it is."

A police siren shrilled outside. The girl's face turned whiter. "I've leveled with you, Shayne. I've told all I know."

The redhead rose as two policemen entered. He indicated the wounded man with a curt nod. "He took a shot at me. Have him fixed up and then let Will Gentry shake him down. See if his tongue's looser then. I'll be in later to lodge a formal complaint."

"Right, Mr. Shayne." The policemen helped the man out.

Shayne turned to Swoboda. She stood up, swaying toward him. "Thanks, redhead."

"We're not through yet, babe."

"No?" She widened her eyes provocatively and moistened her full lips.

"You're not to leave town," he said harshly. "Understand? And I want you to run another seance tonight."

"Why?" She put out her slim hand and touched his cheek gently, invitingly, and moved closer.

"Because I say so," he snapped, picked up his hat and went out the door.

Outside, he leaped into his car and sped to the *News* building. There were no tails behind him and it seemed almost lonesome.

He parked, entered the building, strode through the lobby and took the elevator up to the editorial floor, long-legging it through the desk-filled room till he reached Timothy Rourke's office.

The gangling reporter was typing with two fingers, a green eyeshade on his forehead and a cigarette dangling from a corner of his mouth.

"I'd like to listen to that tape you made last night, Tim," Shayne said.

"O.K." Rourke stopped typing, opened a drawer and handed Shayne the spool.

"Where can we play it back?"

"Here, if you want." Rourke's bony hands swept a clear place on the desk. He rose, lifted a compact recorder-player from a precarious balance on top of a file case, and brought it over. He inserted the spool of tape and plugged it in. They rewound it quickly, then snapped it on "play" and bent together over the machine.

Once again the voice of Madame Swoboda came, rasping and mechanical on the imperfect pick-up. The words were recognizable, however, and the sound intelligible. First the intoned psalm to set the spiritual atmosphere as eerie as it had been last night . . . *He hath done marvelous things* . . . then the message from beyond . . . *Sharon, my marriage was a mistake . . .* and finally Jimsey's voice speaking to Mother and Daddy . . . *it is so far . . . for two hours and thirty-six minutes I have traveled . . . through the forty-eight outer worlds . . . I am happy —but when I lay dying Friday night I spoke your names eight times . . .*

"Same old gobbledegook it was the first time," Rourke observed cynically.

"I'm not so sure it's gobbledegook."

The redhead played it through once more, listening with strained and sober attention. Rourke went back to his typing, looking up as Shayne snapped off the recorder and rose with a faint, grim smile of satisfaction. "Guard that tape with your life, Tim. It might be Exhibit A."

"What's cooking?"

Shayne strode across the room. "Haven't time to explain. Tell your boss to keep the presses open. The *News* might get one hell of an exclusive. Oh— and Tim—" He stopped half through the doorway— "Meet me at Swoboda's a little before eight."

"That tape recording must have been good," Rourke said as the door swung shut.

Shayne stopped at a bar, ordered a double cognac and carried it with a tall glass of ice water to the phone booth where he dialed Will Gentry's private number.

"Did the mug I sent you open up, Will?" he said when the connection was made.

"He *was* open. You did a good job."

"He's not dead, is he?"

"No, just a few shattered ribs."

"What's the dope on him, Will?"

"He's no one on record."

"Who hired him to go gunning for me?"

"A stranger came up to him in a bar and bought him for the tailing job—he said."

"That's the story he told me."

"He really seems to be some sort of screwball independent as he claims," Gentry said. "There's no Syndicate affiliation that we've been able to uncover, at least. He claims he shot at you in self-defense. How about that?"

"Nuts!"

"O.K. Suppose you brief me a little, though. How come it happened in off-hours at a spook house? What was it—a love triangle? Are you courting the Madame?"

"Not exactly, but it's an idea." Shayne paused, took a sip of cognac and followed it with water. "You might have a man at tonight's seance, Will. Just in case."

"Just in case of what? We've checked Madame Swoboda. She's clean."

"Maybe so. I haven't got it all added up yet."

"Well, while you're figuring, I'll keep my men on tap here. By the way, I hear you're in trouble over at the Beach."

"That's nothing unusual. As long as Painter warms the chief's chair, I probably will be."

Gentry chuckled. "All right, Mike. I'll let you know if anything develops here."

Shayne hung up, broke the connection, dropped

in another coin and called his office, finishing the cognac while he waited for Lucy to answer.

"Did Bill Martin call, angel?"

"Yes. There's nothing threatening Clarissa Milford so far."

"I only hope that eager-beaver knows a threat when he sees one," Shayne said somberly. "On his next report, tell him to tail Clarissa when she goes to the seance tonight."

"Are you going, too?"

"Yes, but I think that'll be it. She's closing down."

"Good. No more voodoo threats for anybody— especially you."

"Nobody's put a hex on me."

"Maybe not, but Will Gentry called earlier this afternoon and I know about Swoboda putting that gunman on you."

"Who says it was Swoboda?"

"I do."

"She'll sue you for slander."

"Michael—" her voice grew suddenly small— "please be careful."

"I will, angel. See you later."

He hung up and went out to his car. It was exactly five minutes to five when he arrived at the building which housed the Federal Narcotics Bureau. He parked in front, bounded up the stairs and into the marble lobby, crossing it without slowing his stride. He by-passed the long, wide stairway and long-legged it down the hall.

When he burst through a door at the far end, he found his friend, Steve Crain, standing in the outer office at the water cooler.

"Hello, Mike. What's the rush?" Crain dropped the cup he held in a basket and extended his hand. "I'm about to call it a day. Shall we go down and have a drink?"

Shayne shook his head. "No, let's go into your private office. I'd like some information, and I may have some that will interest you."

Crain led the way down a door-lined corridor to an office at the end. Inside, he motioned Shayne to a chair, closed the glass-paneled door behind them, and tilted back in his own swivel chair, pushing cigarettes and a lighter across the desk to Shayne.

Crain was not what is commonly called a self-made man, but rather a keep-what-you've-got man. A career man in the narcotics service, he had started at the top and stayed there. His face was austere and pale and he regarded Shayne through silver-rimmed glasses with old-fashioned wire hooks over his ears. Shayne had worked with him on previous occasions and had found him capable, honest and intelligent, dedicated to his chosen task of combating the drug traffic.

Shayne crossed his long legs, lit a cigarette and said, "I know you cut off the flow of dope into the Miami area a few months back. Has it stayed cut off?"

Crain's forehead wrinkled. "It's still tight as a drum. We're covering every wharf and inlet. The big operators have either been jailed or run out of

154

town or, as in the case of De Luca, kept under such strict surveillance that they're inoperative." He laughed shortly. "They tell me De Luca's had to hedge by moving into the loan-shark racket."

Shayne nodded. "And very successfully, I believe. So you're sure he's not actively involved at present with narcotics?"

"Absolutely. We've got the Syndicate stopped short here."

"I'm glad to hear it. It confirms my opinion."

"Which is what?"

"That what I have to discuss with you is a wild-cat operation."

Crain frowned. "You think dope is coming in?"

"I'd stake my license on it," Shayne said.

14

The redhead briefed Crain on what he had come to suspect during a day and night's sleuthing.

"If those three sportsmen hadn't become worried about my presence on Sylvester's boat," Shayne said, "and showed it in a number of ways, I might never have suspected anything. They swapped a fish in a jolly drunken way with the men on the Cuban boat, and now I'm convinced they brought in a fish-belly full of dope right under my eyes."

Crain nodded. "It's possible. Since Castro's revolution in Cuba, the stuff has dammed up there. The old smuggling contacts have been broken and it takes time to set up new ones. In the interval, someone from the old regime might well do a little hijacking over there and start a hit-and-run operation of his own."

"Yes. I barged right into the middle of one. At first I thought it was only a screwy batch of fishermen who had chartered Sylvester's boat, but after a while the fast, new, dirtied-up engine they'd put in for him and the way they were keeping him drunk all the time began to bother me. And then, when they murdered him—"

"Too bad," Crain said. "Why do you think they did it?"

"Maybe they thought he had brought me in to check on them, or maybe they thought he knew more than he did. Of course, after they tipped their hands by getting tough with him, he probably did know."

"So then they figured you knew too, and tried to kill you this afternoon at Madame Swoboda's." Crain leaned back and stroked his jaw. "That's the confusing part of it. It would seem that they get their instructions from her, but is that *all* she is— a go-between? If so, it's hard to see why she would be necessary to their enterprise."

"She seemed like an unnecessary complication to me too at first." Shayne snubbed out his cigarette, "But there was cabala—those numbers incorporated in one of her messages."

"Let's hear it."

The redhead leaned back, reciting from memory, "... *for two hours and thirty-six minutes I have traveled through the forty-eight outer worlds ... when I lay dying Friday night I spoke your name eight times ...*"

Crain's pen jerked across the paper. "Two hours and thirty-six minutes. That must have thrown you off at first."

"It did. I tried to relate it to time instead of a point in space—longitude."

"And forty-eight is the latitude of Miami."

Shayne nodded bleakly. "Today is Friday, and very soon it will be eight o'clock and Sylvester's boat—this time without Sylvester—will contact a Cuban boat and receive a gift of another fish with a belly full of dope."

"But the Coast Guard will be there to take it from them." Crain's eyes glowed. "Let's try to put together a little more of what we'll be up against. Those three men were recruited by someone, each for his specialty—"

"That 'someone' still bothers me. I thought it was De Luca at first, but everything points to his noninvolvement. In fact, the more I investigated, the more it became apparent that this was a carefully worked out freelance operation, as much in defiance of the Syndicate as of the law enforcement agencies. Consider how careful the three were to avoid the slightest contact with organized crime down here. They went to scrupulous trouble to provide themselves with sportsmen's identities on Sylvester's boat."

The vertical lines in Shayne's forehead deepened. "Madame Swoboda, when I had her in a tight spot, pretended to level with me—and she did, to a point. But she did it in a way to suggest it was a Syndicate operation—which was one of many things which convinced me it was not. In the first place, as an operation in defiance of the Syndicate, her part in it began to make sense. The men on the boat were all criminals of record—but note that they had never been associated with the narcotics racket before. Just one more little item to remove them from suspicion of either the Syndicate or the police."

"But that involved a way of getting the pick-up information through spirit messages—"

"The shrewdest trick of all. They knew they'd be watched by both the police and local Syndicate representatives, and this way they took no risks of tapped phone wires, opened letters or observed meetings. And still one other thing occurs to me." Shayne's thumb and forefinger gently massaged his left earlobe. His eyes were speculative.

Crain waited.

"Let it ride for the moment," the redhead said. "It's only a hunch and it won't, in any way, affect your operations on the high seas. I'll know in another three hours if I'm right or wrong."

He rose and stood looking down at Crain with a penetrating stare. "Here's what I suggest as a first step. Talk to Peter Painter at the Beach—he's too mule-headed to listen to me—and find out if he's got a police guard on the *Santa Clara*. If he has, get him to take it off. Make it easy for that boat to go out tonight."

"I see." Crain pushed back his chair.

"They'll take a chance on this one last pick-up, I think, figuring to come ashore somewhere far up the coast and then skin out for good, so you'll have to make *your* pick-up good. There won't be another opportunity."

"We'll take care of it. I'd better start making arrangements with the Coast Guard."

A slow grin spread over the detective's lean face.

"Now what have you got up your sleeve?" Crain asked.

"I'm considering making some arrangements of my own. You wouldn't object to wiping out the loan-shark racket in Miami at the same time, would you?"

Crain grinned back. "It's a little out of my line, but if it wouldn't hamper the main operation—"

"Won't hamper it at all. In fact, I'm thinking of enlisting somebody to do the heaviest part of your work for you. It may well be that all the Coast Guard and the Narcotics Bureau will have to do is stand by and pick up the pieces."

"It sounds easy, but I don't get it."

"I'll give you a hint. There's a gentleman once involved in narcotics smuggling who has been forced, as a result of pressures put on him by your office, to take recourse to the loan-shark racket."

"De Luca?"

"Right. So what do you think would happen if he received a discreet tip that somebody was muscling into his old racket and would be at such a place at such a time tonight taking on a cargo?"

"Mayhem!" Crain said. "An absolute massacre." He walked around the desk and clapped Shayne on the shoulder. "Too bad you can't be with us to watch the smoke."

"It is, but I've some voodoo business to clean up

tonight. While you're watching two dope smugglers trying to blast each other's boats out of the water, I'll be listening to Madame Swoboda pull voices out of the Great Beyond."

15

Shayne drew up in front of Madame Swoboda's at quarter to eight and found Tim Rourke batting mosquitoes and waiting for him outside on the damp and sinking flagstones. The same aura of decay hung over the yellow house and the same diffused green glow seeped from beneath the drawn drapes.

A few tourists straggled up the steps. Shayne motioned Tim to wait and followed them to the door, the cloyingly sweet odor catching his nostrils as he neared it. Among the devotees he saw Percy and Mabel Thain, Dan and Clarissa Milford and the thin, gray woman. The redhead met Dan's troubled glance until Dan looked lugubriously away, then suddenly Shayne suppressed a start as a petite girl craned her neck from behind a bulky tourist and gave him a gamin grin. She strolled over to him.

Under his breath Shayne asked, "What in hell are you doing here, Lucy?"

"I came to protect you. Besides, I always wanted to go to a seance."

Shayne snorted and walked back to Rourke. "Lucy's here, of all things. Sit next to her at the table, Tim, and keep an eye on her, will you?"

"You're expecting fireworks, I judge."

"Maybe. Anyway, do what I say."

"I will. But this is the one hell of a hard way to write a story. I don't even know why you wanted Swoboda to hold another seance tonight."

"For the obvious reason—to keep her on tap for police questioning after the Coast Guard and Steve Crain have cleaned up the *Santa Clara* affair. Also, there's the voodoo angle. I thought this might provide an opportunity for the person who is threatening Clarissa Milford to reveal himself."

"You know who it is yet?"

"No, but I've sorted some of it out. I'm pretty sure there's no connection between the threat to Clarissa Milford and the things that happened on Sylvester's boat. And I know De Luca's involvement with the Milfords. But the voodoo doll is still as live a threat to Clarissa Milford as it was to Henlein."

"A live threat ending in death maybe?"

"Let's hope not." Shayne looked at his watch. "Things ought to be popping pretty soon in the forty-eight outer worlds."

"By the way," Rourke said, "my office has a helicopter within telescopic sight of the *Santa Clara*. We ought to get the feed-back about the time we get out of the seance."

"Good. Let's go in now."

On the rickety steps, Rourke asked, "Are you going to tell Dan Milford you've pulled De Luca's heat off him? He looks like death warmed over tonight."

Shayne shook his head. "I'm letting it ride until after the seance. I don't want to risk upsetting the balance. If anybody has anything planned, I want it to go on—as planned."

In the narrow hallway a little crowd of people was dammed up in front of the sliding doors to the seance room. Shayne moved close to Clarissa and said, in a guarded voice, "Sit next to me at the table."

The crowd was larger than last night and there was a delay while the secretary with the brown horn-rimmed glasses brought more chairs. When the doors were finally opened Shayne pushed forward into the nearly dark room and, by holding fast to Clarissa Milford and ignoring the rights of others, managed to locate himself at the table directly across from Madame Swoboda. Dan Milford took a chair on the other side of his wife and Percy Thain sat at Shayne's left.

As before, Madame Swoboda sat erect in an armless chair, one hand flat on the table on each side of the palely-lit green ball. As before, her eyes were open, fastened unblinkingly on a point ahead, the eerie light shining upward into her face. She wore the same silver gossamer veils trailing from the tiara on her head. Behind her, the unadorned cabinet was closed and the windows draped in funereal black velvet.

Her showmanship was perfect and her beauty appeared more ethereal now than sensual.

When everyone was seated and the last whisper of noise had died away, Madame Swoboda spoke in the darkened room.

"For those new among us . . . link your own thumbs. Link the little finger of each hand with that of the person beside you. The circle travels, never ending . . . Wait . . . wait . . . wait . . . The journey is long . . . We stand in a timeless void . . . The spirits resolve out of space and nothingness . . ."

A rustling went around the table as they found each other's hands and linked fingers. Then the hushed quiet settled in again.

He hath done marvelous things . . . His right hand and His holy arms . . . Three times she intoned the Ninety-eighth Psalm, her voice weirdly monotonous in the dark.

After another silence she closed her eyes. Although Shayne knew the performance was trickery, he could not help admiring the conviction with which she did it. Almost visibly her mind seemed to be willing the spirits to speak.

She shivered and then was quiet. Her face above the weird green light might have been carved from stone.

Words came from her almost unmoving lips: "I am getting vibrations for someone who has suffered a loss. If the bereaved person is among us, let him listen. . . ."

165

Silence again.

Finally, from high in the room a thin voice came, nearly inaudible at first, but gradually growing louder: "Daddy . . . Daddy . . . Daddy . . ."

Shayne felt both Clarissa and Percy Thain tighten their fingers on his.

Percy said, "Jimsey!" in an agonized voice.

"Do you hear me, Daddy?" The thin spirit voice spoke again.

"I hear you, Jimsey! I hear you, son! Who killed you?" The words were wrenched forth in almost unbearable anguish.

The child voice continued: "I am strong enough to tell you now . . . I was murdered, Daddy. *She* did it. . . ."

"Who *is* she, son?" Thain whispered intensely.

In wan and dreary complaint, the voice went on. "She was driving on the back road. . . . She was going fast. . . . She killed me, Daddy, and she deserves to die." There was a long silence. Then, "Let her admit her guilt now and clear her soul."

Abruptly, the green light in front of Madame Swoboda went out.

In the new and total dark, everyone was completely blind. The circle broke. Chairs scraped as they were pushed back. Bodies bumped into bodies, hands brushed faces, shins knocked against chairs.

Percy Thain, at Shayne's left, jerked back and rose from the table, but Shayne still held his finger-grip with Clarissa. For an instant the redhead speculated on the sheer animal terror which pervaded the

166

room, then he put his arms around Clarissa and pulled her with quick force from her chair. Alarmed, she cried out. Shayne clamped his big hand over her face and gripped her firmly as she struggled against him.

At nearly the same instant at his near right, there was a curious "punging" sound, and then a small clatter.

He made an exploring sweep with one arm in the darkness behind him, but he was hampered by Clarissa's closeness. At the end of the long table a match was struck and the tiny flame of a candle grew in the dark.

Madame Swoboda screamed. Mouth agape, she stood in the flickering light beside the opened door of the cabinet, her eyes fixed on the candle in a catatonic stare.

It was black.

A black candle was for death.

Shayne's glance slashed around the room. In the candle's first morbid glow everyone stood as though impaled. To his right, at the place where Clarissa had been sitting, a knife lay on the table. The point of its blade was broken off and embedded near the table edge.

A black candle was for death . . . and someone, tonight, had meant death for Clarissa!

Now they were all looking at the broken knife. Someone screamed again, and someone whimpered. In a moment of unified, breathless horror each viewed the instrument of intended death, and then seemed to shun knowledge of it—as if to admit its existence would be to invite it to fulfill its purpose on him.

Mabel Thain stood beside her shaken husband, tears starting from her eyes as she stared at Clarissa. Clarissa's face was like parchment, her expression dazed and disbelieving. Dan Milford bent over her where she had slumped into Shayne's chair, his eyes wild and desperate.

Shayne barked, "Don't move! Everyone stay exactly where you are!"

He walked to the end of the table, picked up the flickering black candle and carried it back to set it beside the knife.

"Who lit that candle?" Milford demanded hoarsely.

"It was a mistake," Madame Swoboda said. "I couldn't see which one I took in the dark."

"It doesn't matter," Shayne said. "Someone tried to kill Mrs. Milford with a knife, not a candle."

In the uncertain light, the redhead looked at the knife. The handle was bound in gauze; no fingerprints would show. From its shape, he judged it to be a common kitchen knife, the size between paring and carving—not too short a blade to reach the heart, not too large to be easily concealed. The point was broken off two-thirds of the way down. Had it been thrown or thrust?

Shayne straightened, his hard, appraising glance moving from face to face. Everyone looked shocked and guilty—even Lucy. Mabel Thain was sobbing openly, her arms around Clarissa, her face buried against her sister's shoulder.

His glance held on Madame Swoboda. "Where's the fuse box that controls the lights in this room?"

"In the basement, on the left beside the stairway."

Tremblingly she took another candle from the cabinet and lit it, careful this time to select a pink one. She met Shayne with it halfway around the table. "You can get there through the kitchen." She had mastered her first fright and uncertainty. Her voice was firm.

"You show me. I want you to come with me." Shayne paused at the sliding doors. "I'm putting Mr. Rourke in charge to see that no one leaves."

He waited a moment to let the words take effect, then followed Madame Swoboda down a narrow hall. The candle threw guttering shadows about them. They passed a wall telephone and came to the kitchen. On the hall-side an apparently new ornamental grillwork had been fitted into the wall above the kitchen door. Inside the kitchen, Shayne frowned as his gray eyes ranged bleakly around the shadowed room. His knobby hand jerked toward a padlocked cabinet high against the ceiling on the other side of the grillwork.

"What's in there?"

Madame Swoboda hesitated for only a second before she opened a drawer, took out a single key and handed it to him. An open household stepladder stood in a corner by the stove. Shayne strode over and scraped the short ladder across the cracked linoleum to the kitchen doorway.

Standing on the second step of the ladder, he unlocked the cabinet door. Inside was what he had expected to find—a tape recorder placed in front of the open grillwork to let sound issue into the hall, and from there into the seance room through another grillwork against the ceiling.

"The source of your astral voices?" he asked wryly.

Madame Swoboda nodded, opened her mouth to speak and then seemed to think better of it.

Shayne stepped off the ladder and ran taut fingers through his wiry hair.

"It wasn't the tape I prepared for tonight," Madame Swoboda said suddenly.

"Whose tape was it?"

"I don't know."

"Are you trying to make me believe the tape we heard tonight was substituted for the one you prepared, and you don't know who did it?"

"Yes. Don't be too smart for your own good, Shayne. What possible reason would I have for accusing a client of murder? I'm in this to make a living."

"Who said it was a client who was accused?"

She stared, visibly disconcerted. "Why—I don't know. It seems obvious, though. Someone did try to stab Mrs. Milford."

"We'll come back to that. Where are the stairs to the basement?"

Holding the candle high, she led the way through

a door and down a sagging flight of stairs. A darkness pervaded the air. At the bottom, she stooped and pointed to the fuse box.

The redhead walked over. On a short wire leading to the fuse box a small, square metal box had been inserted. Dropping some melted wax on a shelf, he made the candle secure and examined the small box. It was a timer set to break the electrical circuit at eight-twelve. A simple mechanism, but dependable. Whoever had put it there knew Madame Swoboda's promptness in starting the seances. Whoever had put it there wanted the inky darkness upstairs at exactly eight-twelve.

Carefully, using his handkerchief to minimize the smearing of any fingerprints that might be on it, Shayne removed the timer and reconnected the wire to the fuse box. As the electricity went on, he heard the slight rasp of the tape recorder near the head of the stairs in the kitchen. No more voices were issuing from it.

He turned. "Who put this timer on the fuse box?"

"I've no idea," Madame Swoboda said tautly. "I don't even know what a timer is."

"It's what made the lights go out."

"Well, I didn't do it certainly, for the same reason I didn't record that tape that came on tonight. I like to make a living. Probably whoever substituted his tape for mine put that gadget on the wire too."

"Maybe. Come back upstairs."

In the long hall under a low-watt electric bulb, Shayne stopped and reached for the telephone.

Madame Swoboda's voice came on an indrawn breath of stark protest. "You're not going to call the police?"

"Why not? Somebody tried to murder Clarissa Milford."

"Shayne!" Her hand gripped his arm fiercely. "I didn't do it! I know nothing about it!"

"Then you've nothing to fear from the police."

"You know I can't stand a police investigation!"

"Do I?"

"I had absolutely no reason for wanting to murder Clarissa Milford—"

"Tell that to the police."

"But it looks bad for me. They'll hold me for questioning at least overnight, won't they?"

"Probably."

"That's too long! I've got to get out of here. Now!"

"Why?"

"For personal reasons. They have nothing at all to do with tonight's seance." She was pressing close to him, desperately intense, pleading, her breath warm on his face. "Do something for me, Shayne, please! You can't lose by it."

"Can I gain?"

"Yes, whatever you want. Just let me get out of here before the police come, or if you can't do that because of your professional reputation, smooth it out for me with them. Fix it so they'll let me go right away." Her voice grew husky, seductive. "Will you do that, Shayne?"

He smiled wryly. "I still can't see what I'll gain."

She lifted her hand suddenly, tore off the tiara and the enshrouding veil and threw them to the floor. As her arm descended, her bracelet caught in the silver shawl, pulling it down and exposing one perfect breast. She pressed close to him, her voice caressing. "Shayne, I'll be good to you. There's time for that. That fire you wondered about— I'll burn you in a way you won't forget."

Shayne said harshly, "You have burned me—with rage!"

She reached for him with her lips. "What are you saying?"

"I'm saying that your three associates murdered Sylvester!"

"I know nothing of that."

"You know. Is the reason you have to leave town so fast because you don't trust them? Are you afraid they'll cut you out of your share?"

"Share of what? I don't know what you're talking about."

"I'm talking about the last pick-up Ed Woodbine, Slim Collins and Vince Becker are going to make tonight from a Cuban boat. They're out on Sylvester's boat. I'm talking about narcotics in a fish belly. They were probably to meet you later up the coast. But if you aren't there, they'll go on without you and then you'll never get your share. I'm talking about Slug Murphy, Slim Rizzo and Joe Arminetti!"

She stood very still, her head drawn back, staring at him penetratingly with her gray, hypnotic eyes. "All right." Her voice was precise, cool and under control. "I don't know how you know, but you do know some of it. It's only the smallest part. You leave me no choice, so I'm going to tell you the rest, and then I'm going to make you a proposition—the best you ever had in your life."

"I've had some good ones."

"Not this good. So listen, Shayne. You're right about tonight. If I'm not there they'll move on and try to cut me out. What you don't know is that my part is the lion's share."

"I assumed that. And I know that Swoboda is nobody's dupe, nobody's hired go-between. Swoboda is the brains and master of the whole operation."

She gasped. "Who told you?"

"No one. It figures. Otherwise why this run-around of passing on information through numbers incorporated in spirit messages? If this was your project, if you recruited those three men for the job, then you had to have some way of keeping the reins tight in your hands. You'd have to make sure *you'd* be the one to receive the vital information that came in from your outside contact. This seance set-up gave you complete control. You could with-hold time-and-place information on the next pick-up until you had assured yourself the previous ship-ment had progressed through Miami according to plan to the ultimate receiving or cutting center."

"All right. Here's the rest of it. I told you it was Vegas where all this started. It wasn't—it was Cuba. I did a mentalist act there, but I also had a small part in a narcotics ring operated by the Syndicate

174

with a nod from someone in the Batista govern-ment. Then when Castro strong-armed Batista out, everything fell to pieces and through a lucky break I got my hands on some of the stuff. The problem was to get it to the States, so I flew around the country and lined up my operation, using contacts I'd made when I was working with the Syndicate."

"You must have been pretty afraid the Syndicate would find out."

"I was, believe me. More than of the police. That's why I had to keep it tight in my hands at all costs. That's why I set up this seance business."

She paused for a moment, and when she spoke again her voice was charged with hoarse intensity. "So, here's my proposition. There's more of that golden stuff than came in tonight. We've only brought in six shipments. I can cut those three goons out, Shayne, if I can get to my contact up north quick enough, and *I can cut you in*. Even money. And you can leave Miami with me and pro-tect your interests all the way. And Shayne—" her voice softened—"I'm part of the bargain, for as long as you want." She pulled his head down and pressed her lips on his mouth searingly.

He let the kiss end, then pulled away, "Sorry. The Coast Guard has already picked up your three stooges from the *Santa Clara* and seized the ship-ment, and the Syndicate now knows about you, and so will the police when I put through this call."

"You bastard!" She swung away from him, seeth-ing. "You police-stool bastard!" She lifted her hand, ostensibly to pull the silver shawl over her bare

175

breast, but when it reappeared something in it flickered metallically in the dim hall light.

Shayne's big hand moved in the same instant. He wrenched the delicate lady's gun from her grasp. It clattered to the floor. With a sob in her throat, she bent. Her hand snaked out. Shayne stamped his foot on it, and before the cry of pain had fully left her lips, had the gun in his own hand.

With it trained on her, he reached for the telephone and dialed the number of Police Headquarters.

16

When Will Gentry was on the line, Shayne said, "Better come over to Swoboda's fast, Will."

"Why?"

"I'll tell you in a minute. Did you get any reports yet on the affair of the *Santa Clara?*"

"They just came in. De Luca and some out-of-town hoods poured it into each other and then the Coast Guard and the Narcotics Bureau mopped up. Wait a minute! Is what you've got at Swoboda's part of that?"

"The biggest part. But there's something else that isn't related to the smuggling. You should have had a man at the seance tonight the way I told you. Someone made an attempt on Clarissa Milford's life."

"Well, I'm damned! If you knew they were going to, why didn't you insist?"

"I didn't know for sure. I'm not psychic."

"The way you've been hanging out there lately, you seem to—" Gentry stopped abruptly. "Milford? Is that the Clarissa Milford who was in the news

177

last week? That freak accident? Her car was stolen and her nephew killed by it?"

"That's the one. Only I don't think it was an accident. I think it was murder. Do me a favor, Will—"

"Do *me* one," Gentry snapped. "Tell me in plain English what's up."

"I think I can wrap it up fast," Shayne said, "if you'll take Mr. and Mrs. Milford and Mr. and Mrs. Thain in for questioning along with whoever else you want. And give me about an hour before you turn them loose."

"All right," Gentry said grudgingly. "We'll be right over."

Shayne took Madame Swoboda back to the others in the seance room and waited for the police. The medium seemed to have lost all her fire. She slumped into her chair at the head of the table and sat staring dully ahead.

As soon as Gentry arrived with two policemen, Shayne left with Lucy. He headed the car toward the northwest outskirts of the city where the twin houses of Milfords and Thains stood in the scraggly field.

The night was foggy and moonless and the damp air had a desolate feel. Its heaviness separated people, set up a barrier between them, isolated each individual in a gray world of fog. Shayne extended his right arm and drew Lucy across the seat until her shoulder rested against his chest. That was a little better. The night lost some of its feeling of desolation.

The trenches were deep in the redhead's lean face. He lit a cigarette, took a deep drag, tossed the dead match out the window and said, "I'm taking you along, angel, because I've got a feeling I can use your woman's eye." He paused, asking after a moment, "Lucy, did you notice anything strange about that tape recording tonight?"

She stirred under his sheltering arm. "Of course. It was darned strange. Who'd murder a child? Jimsey wasn't heir to a fortune or anything."

"That isn't what I mean. He was only twelve when he died. At that age children, especially boys, are quite attached to their mothers. Yet, instead of saying 'Mother and Daddy' as he did the night before, he called only for 'Daddy' tonight."

"That *is* strange."

"Now the point is," Shayne removed his arm from her shoulder, ran one hand quickly through his wiry hair, then put it back around her, "Madame Swoboda made the previous recordings and she did the natural thing—had Jimsey call for both parents. But whoever made tonight's tape either knew that Jimsey was *not* attached to his mother, or knew nothing about Jimsey or twelve-year-old boys in general. What's your choice?"

"That Jimsey wasn't attached to Mabel. She's not exactly the mother type—and whoever made the tape knew it."

"That's what I think." Shayne stared bleakly into the saffron glow the car lights made in the fog.

"There are so many loose ends," Lucy murmured. "How does D. L. come into it, for instance?

Is it possible he sent someone to kill Clarissa so that her husband would get her insurance and be able to pay his debt?"

"It's possible. But voodoo dolls and seances seem too roundabout for a gangster. De Luca's men don't spend time trying to scare people to death. We'd do better to concentrate on the others who had a motive for killing Clarissa."

"You mean her husband? And Percy and Mabel Thain?"

"Yes."

"It's hard for me to see why it would have been any of them, Michael."

"It's coming clearer," Shayne said.

He turned in at the Milford driveway, stopped the car and helped Lucy out. Together they walked around to the back. The kitchen door was open as Clarissa had said it always was. Shayne switched on a light. A few unwashed dishes lay in the sink, a pot of cold coffee stood on the stove. Nothing here told anything.

They walked through the small dining el into the living room. A tape recorder stood on the table. When Shayne connected it, the rhythmic beat of piano boogie sounded. He switched it off and moved across the room to look at two miniatures hanging on the wall; one of Clarissa as a young girl, the other, undoubtedly of her sister, Mabel, as ugly then as she was now.

They covered the rest of the house quickly. The two bedrooms were small, each contained a double bed and two dressers, and revealed nothing of interest. Shayne went down the basement steps, leaving Lucy alone in the living room, but there was nothing to tell him anything there either.

Turning off the lights and closing the kitchen door, they went out to the car, drove down the Milford driveway, still shrouded in fog, and up the next drive to the Thain house.

The kitchen here was identical, but neater. The pots and pans sparkled; the stove and icebox were spotless.

"This is curious, Michael." Lucy had opened one of the cupboards. "The dishes seem new. There's a complete set—eight of everything. All the same."

"What's curious about it, angel?"

"There aren't even any odd glasses," she said. "Everyone I know uses a few jelly glasses to eke out."

"I still don't get it."

"If Jimsey was twelve," Lucy said, "we can assume that Mabel and Percy Thain have been married at least thirteen years. By that time the average housewife has broken up several sets of dishes. But she always hangs on to a few of them, just in case. It looks here as if Mabel must have thrown everything out lately and bought all new stuff."

Remembering the austere woman with the pinched, unhappy mouth and bony finger, Shayne said, "Maybe she's just careful and never breaks anything. She looks it."

In the living room the unimaginative furniture looked new and unused too. Under the shiny desk stood a wastebasket with a few torn letters and some crumpled paper in it. Dumping its contents on the immaculate floor, Shayne sifted through it.

Lucy turned at his low whistle. "What is it, Michael?"

Shayne's blunt fingers held out a piece of torn cellophane. "Wrappings from a tape that would fit the recording machine we saw at Milfords'."

"What of it? Mabel and Clarissa must have seen a lot of each other."

"It's only a supposition. But if you think back you'll remember that Percy Thain was the only one who spoke during the seance. He seemed to know when the pauses were due. And the tape answered him pretty accurately."

Lucy nodded, her eyes quickening with excitement. "You think he made the tape and switched it for the one on Madame Swoboda's machine, and put the timer on the fuse box to turn off the lights?"

"It's possible."

"So he tried to kill Clarissa because he thought Clarissa ran over his son—"

"I wonder." Shayne lit a cigarette and took a deep drag. "You asked earlier what motive there'd be for deliberately killing a child. Why should Clarissa have wanted to?"

"Maybe she didn't. Maybe it was an accident."

Shayne scowled. "Percy might have suspected that Clarissa ran over Jimsey, but he wasn't sure. That's obviously the reason he made the tape—in the hope of forcing her to admit it." The scowl eased, but the redhead's gaunt face remained sober.

When he had left these houses last night, Shayne had sensed that no one except possibly Dan Milford actually believed in the seances. Certainly, if Percy Thain had prepared the tape used tonight with the supposed voice of Jimsey on it, he knew that the seances were faked. Why, then, had he and Mabel attended them every night since Jimsey's death?

The answer came almost at once. Percy Thain thought Clarissa believed in the seances. The voodoo doll was the opening gun; then the tape and the timer set on the fuse box to cut the lights. Thain had counted on pyramiding fear to force a confession from Clarissa. It was the kind of unrewarding plan a man mad with grief might conceive of.

If, indeed, it had been Thain who left Clarissa the voodoo doll and who had made tonight's recording. It *could* have been Clarissa's husband, Dan. It could have been her sister, Mabel Thain. It even could have been Clarissa herself, though the motivation for that was obscure.

Shayne snubbed out his cigarette in a spotlessly clean dish and said abruptly, "Come on, Lucy. Let's finish going through the house before they come home."

In the first bedroom a picture of Mabel stood on the man's dresser, a picture of Percy on the vanity. The second was a boy's room, brown corduroy bedspread on the single bed, a school banner on the wall, a desk with a student's lamp over it, a baseball bat standing in the corner. But it was all too clean and neat. It was silent and sad. Even under

Mabel's compulsively precise housekeeping, some aura of the live boy would have emerged, but none was here now. The room, like the boy, was dead.

Without the touch of his eager, grimy hands, his possessions were static. They were not just waiting to be used; they lay heavily, never to be moved again. The bed was made forever, the bat would stand there until the end of time. There was no feeling that in a moment the boy would stamp into the room, hurl his coat on the bed, seize the bat and rush out to join his companions on the field.

In this room everything had ended.

On the bureau beside a comb, brush and mirror accurately lined up, were two pictures in identical frames. One was obviously a picture of Jimsey. The other was that of a young and smiling soft-haired woman.

Lucy stared silently at the pictures. The resemblance between the two was striking.

A scowl of speculation crossed Shayne's craggy face. "Too old to be his sister," he murmured. "Perhaps this is one of the answers. Suppose Mabel was not Jimsey's real mother? Clarissa didn't say."

"Maybe that's why the dishes are all new. Maybe Percy and Mabel haven't been married long enough to break any." Lucy turned. "If Jimsey were Percy's son, not Mabel's, does that put a new light on things?"

"At least it explains why Percy had Jimsey call only for 'Daddy' on tonight's tape—*if* Percy made that tape."

184

Lucy moved toward the door. "Let's get out of here, Michael."

When Shayne spoke, his voice was hoarse, as if it had not been used for a long while. "That room sort of gets you, doesn't it?"

Lucy nodded.

"You see, I did need your woman's eye."

"Do you suppose," Lucy asked, "you'll ever need the rest of the woman?"

"Angel," he said softly, "I wouldn't be surprised."

17

Shayne and Lucy waited in the car for the Milfords and Thains to come home. The air was still thick with fog. It was a green and heavy night, desolate in feel and in promise, for now that Shayne was so close to the truth, now that the case had been worked through almost to its end, the final act was a sad and distasteful one.

Willfully, he thought of Clarissa: of her calm abiding beauty, of her tenacious will to keep her husband despite the fact that she had believed for a while that he had stopped loving her. He saw the knife broken off in the seance table at the place where Clarissa had been sitting and thought how delicate the line between life and death had been for her tonight.

By the time the lights of the Thains' approaching car made a yellow haze in the fog as it turned in the driveway, Shayne's concentration on Clarissa had served its purpose. The edge of pity had been dulled. The job before him would be easier done.

At the beginning he had sifted through many reasons why Clarissa had been threatened: because her husband needed money; because she had frightened Madame Swoboda by saying she would turn her over to the police; because what a loan-shark racketeer lends must be returned, either in legal tender or in flesh; because Percy Thain believed she had killed his son—but none of them were the right reasons. There was only one "right" one, and it should have been obvious from the start.

When the Thain car with its four passengers stopped, Shayne and Lucy walked over.

"What are you doing here?" Percy Thain asked truculently.

"I'd like to talk to you all a few minutes."

"We were going to retire," Mabel Thain murmured. "We've been through a lot tonight."

"I know. I'll be brief." Shayne's voice was gentle. "I want to ask your husband a question or two."

"Then come in," she said gravely. Her haunted glance included Lucy, and the Milfords.

She led them into the sterile living room. While they were still standing, Shayne turned to Percy Thain. "Did your wife know you put the timer on the electrical circuit tonight at Madame Swoboda's?"

Thain's eyes widened and, infinitesimally, his head lowered, as if to avoid a blow. "I did not—" he began.

"Did she also know you made the recording of Jimsey's voice for tonight's seance?"

Thain raised his head hostilely, but did not answer.

Shayne turned to Mabel, demanding, "Did you know?"

Mabel took two quick steps to stand tense and still beside her husband. "What horrible things are you saying?" Her sunken mouth twisted as though she were about to cry.

Shayne continued implacably, "Is it your opinion your sister was driving her car the night your son was hit by it?"

"How could I believe that about my sister?" Mabel's voice quavered. "Everyone loves Clarissa. She has always been so beautiful, and so lucky— all her life. She would never have been unlucky enough to be the one driving the car when our son was—killed."

"Was he your son, Mrs. Thain?"

She looked stricken. "I—loved him as my son."

Dan Milford, standing with one arm around Clarissa, turned brooding, savage eyes on Shayne. "Let her alone!" The words seemed to be wrenched from him. "Let Mabel alone. She's stood enough!"

Ignoring him, Shayne looked again at Percy Thain. "Please answer my first question. You might as well because no matter how careful you were when you installed the tape and the fuse box cut-off at Swoboda's, the police will find finger-prints."

"All right!" Thain looked desperate and harried. "I made the tape and I installed the timer—and Mabel knew. But it wasn't a crime," he added defensively. "I wanted to find out who killed my son.

188

I had a right to know. I thought I might frighten someone into the admission—"

"Someone? You mean Clarissa?"

"Yes, if she did it! Yes!" Thain shouted.

Clarissa moaned and buried her head on Dan's shoulder.

"She didn't," Shayne said. "Your wife killed him."

"No!" It was an involuntary, uncomprehending denial from Dan Milford.

Thain gasped. His head shook with a rapid palsy.

"It isn't true," Mabel whispered.

"It can't be true," Percy said.

"It is true," Shayne said softly. "And it's even worse than what you thought Clarissa did, because it wasn't an accident—it was murder."

Percy's head kept nodding. For a moment he faced his wife with a look so fathomless and full of hatred that Shayne glanced away.

"Why?" Dan Milford asked. "Why would she want to—"

"She couldn't stand sharing her husband with his son."

"It's a lie," Mabel sobbed, ". . . a lie—"

Shayne stepped close to Mabel and lifted her quavering chin with his blunt fingers. "Clarissa knew, didn't she?" he asked softly. "Clarissa knew you were driving the car that killed Jimsey. And that's why you tried to frighten her—at first with the voodoo doll, and then, when you saw she wasn't going to be scared out of town, you had to try to kill her. It was easier after you had killed the gangster, Henny Henlein—"

"Henny Henlein?" Dan Milford repeated incredulously. "What could Mabel have had to do with him?"

"Henlein must have found out she was driving the car that killed Jimsey. Maybe he had come out here to frighten Clarissa on orders from De Luca and he witnessed the crime. Did he try to blackmail you, Mabel?"

"So that's what you wanted the money for!" Percy Thain shouted madly. "Liar! Murderess!" He lifted his hand as if to strike her, but midway the sobs burst, bending him double and racking his slight body.

"Henlein was killed with his own gun," Shayne said.

"No," Mabel said piteously, cowering from her husband. "No. I was looking in Dan's drawer for money—I was looking everywhere—I was desperate —and I found the gun and took it."

"I know. Dan had taken it away from Henlein. He was having trouble with him, too."

Mabel continued in a kind of sad crooning, as if no one else had spoken. "I knew I'd never get the money to pay him off—from Percy—or anyone. So I knew I'd have to kill him. The dolls didn't scare him off. He made me meet him. It was easy because he didn't think a woman would do it . . ."

"I'll have to take you to Police Headquarters," Shayne said.

She seemed calmed by the sound of his voice. Her sobbing stopped. "I tried," she said numbly. "I tried very hard with Jimsey, but I couldn't love him. He was someone else's child, not mine, and neither Jimsey nor Percy would ever let me forget it. He was Percy's child, and Percy was mine, but Jimsey wasn't mine and I wasn't Jimsey's. He took Percy away from me—"

"You fool!" Percy's eyes were wild and tormented. "You never had me. I wanted a housekeeper. Only a housekeeper. And I married you to get one."

"Percy thought Clarissa ran over Jimsey," Mabel said, seeming not to have heard the shouted insults, seeming only tenuously related to anything that was happening now. "But Clarissa knew *I* did it, because we both knew where she hid the extra set of keys."

"Shall we go now?" Shayne asked gently.

Mabel continued as though he hadn't spoken: "Clarissa told the police she was here with me when it happened—to protect me, you know—but I had already told Percy she wasn't, so that Percy would think she killed Jimsey.

"You see, it had to be either Clarissa or me, because we were the only ones who knew exactly when Jimsey would be coming home from school and which road he took. He always came a back way. Percy was at the office in the daytime and Dan was somewhere downtown and neither of them knew."

She sighed. "The gangster doesn't matter, but I'm sorry about Jimsey now."

"Sorry!" Percy repeated dully.

"I'm glad I didn't kill Clarissa, too," Mabel said, still in the same monotone, "but I had to try because she *knew* and someday she might have told Percy and I wanted Percy to love me."

"Love you! You fool!" Percy breathed.

Mabel seemed to hear nothing but her own voice. "I'd have missed Clarissa," she crooned. "Pretty Clarissa. We live so close and we're always together. But I had to try to kill her because I was afraid . . . and I wanted Percy to love me."

"Get your coat now, Mabel," Shayne said. "It's getting chilly out. We'll go downtown together and Clarissa will come to see you tomorrow."

"When I was little," she said, "I used to try to wear Clarissa's things, because I thought they'd make me pretty, too." She walked obediently to a closet and took out a long, black coat. "This used to be Clarissa's, but it went out of style and she gave it to me."

"How lucky you were," Shayne said, "that you and Clarissa were the same type and you could wear her clothes."

She seemed to hear him then, and for the first time since he had met her, she smiled.